GOLD RUSH RUNAWAY

GOLD RUSH RUNAWAY

A Historical Novel of
Alaska Exploration and Adventure

Douglas DeVries

**Young Adult
Historical Fiction**

JADE RAM

3003 Wendy's Way #9
Anchorage, Alaska
99517-1466

Production by

PO Box 221974 Anchorage, Alaska 99522-1974

Hard Cover ISBN 1-877721-04-2
Soft Cover ISBN 1-877721-03-4

Library of Congress Catalog Card Number: 97-69457

Manufactured in the United States of America.

GOLD RUSH RUNAWAY is dedicated to the memory of the men and women who, in the late 1890s, "opened up" Alaska for those who now enjoy its aura and grandeur:

To the memory of Captain Edwin Glenn, for whom the Glenn Highway is named; of Lieutenant Joseph Castner, who led the trail cutting expedition that became the highway; of the men, military and civilian, who worked at the trail cutting; of the natives who worked with and provided sustenance for Lieutenant Castner and his men.

To the memory of those who, during the gold rush heyday, came and stayed to make Alaska their homes, and a place of welcome for us who followed them through the past century.

Douglas DeVries

CONTENTS

I thank my friends for support and encouragement during my writing of Gold Rush Runaway, with special thanks to the following:

Writer friends at the Children's Writer Conference in Fairbanks in August 1997, for insisting that I have a youthful protagonist in my story.

The members of our monthly Children's Writers Group in Anchorage, for their continuing support.

Paula Lindstam, for her caring critique and editing of the manuscript.

To Lyman L. Woodman (deceased), editor of *Lieutenant Castner's Alaskan Exploration*, 1898, whose work provided the interest and inspiration for my book.

To the Cook Inlet Historical Society and its secretary, William Davis, for permission to use quotations and maps from Castner's book in *Gold Rush Runaway*.

To Evan Swensen and Publication Consultants for their work in the layout and publication of this book.

Douglas DeVries

Part One

DECEPTION

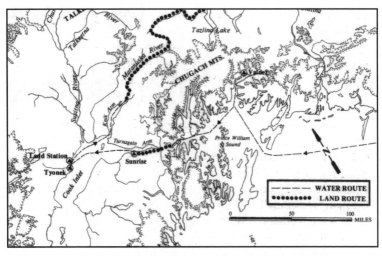

From Haines to Prince William Sound,
to camp on the site of present day Whittier,
across Portage Glacier and on to Sunrise
and Hope on the Turnagain Arm of Cook Inlet,
by boat to Tyonek and Ladd's Station,
and into the Knik Arm of Cook Inlet,
April to June, 1898.

I

STEADY throbbing of the engine and rocking of the *Valencia* as it steamed northward through Puget Sound lulled Sven Olafsen to sleep.

After a night and morning of tension he relaxed. From early evening he had watched and waited until the cabin darkened before he sneaked on board. He curled his willowy body within a coil of rope and pulled a tarpaulin over himself. Through the morning hours he feared discovery as men rushing for Alaska's gold fields swarmed aboard. He feared discovery as soldiers, arriving that afternoon of April 7, 1898, crowded on deck. He listened to shouting, swearing, arguing; to boxes and bundles thumping down; to shoes tromping close to his hiding place. He prayed until, underway and undiscovered, he slept.

"Oof." Air forced out of Sven awakened him. Something heavy pinned him to the deck. He pushed against the weight.

"Drat it all." He heard someone swear and the weight shifted. "Who's under there?"

"Get off. Let me sleep." Sven acted as if he belonged there.

Cool evening air chilled him as the tarpaulin was pulled away. He stared up into the probing blue eyes of a tall army lieutenant with light brown hair and a blond moustache.

"Get up." The lieutenant reached down, grabbed Sven's hair and yanked him to his feet.

"Ow." Sven raked his fingers through his tangled blond hair. He tottered on his stiff cramped legs and stretched.

"Are you a stowaway?" the lieutenant, holding Sven at arm's length, asked.

"Oh, no, Sir." Sven felt blood rush to his pale cheeks.

"Why are you hiding here?"

"I wasn't hiding, Sir. I needed a dark, quiet place to sleep." Sven's quick wit helped.

The hint of a smile curled the corner of the lieutenant's lip. "You'd better go find your father."

"That's what I intend to do," Sven said. "He's in Circle City."

"Circle City?" The lieutenant scrutinized the tall, thin, smooth-faced youth clad in brown canvas trousers and wool plaid shirt.

"Yes, Sir. That's where I'm going."

"What's your name?"

"Sven."

"Sven what? What's your surname?"

"Johanson," he lied, and his face became warmer. His parents had taught him to tell the truth. "Who are you, Sir?"

"I am Lieutenant Castner, Joseph Castner, of the United States Army." The lieutenant stood straighter, taller with pride in his military position, as he answered. "Are you a runaway?"

"Oh, no, Sir." Sven face grew hot as Lt. Castner stared into his pale blue eyes. He looked down and bit his lower lip.

"Hmm." With his fingers Lt. Castner lifted Sven's chin. "Hmm."

"'Cuse me, Sir. I have to ... nature calls." Sven grabbed his duffel bag from beneath the tarpaulin and, looking for a new hiding place, walked toward the stern.

He glanced back as he ducked behind a mound of miners' supplies. Stroking his chin, eyes narrowed, Lt. Castner watched him. Sven crouched and weaved his way among stacks of tarpaulin covered boxes. When he felt safe he sank to the deck, leaned back, closed his eyes and prayed.

"You, Boy, get away from there." A burly, dark-eyed man towered over Sven. "Nobody steals while I'm watching."

Sven twisted away as the man aimed a kick at him. "Sorry."

He scrambled to his feet and hurried to the rail before stopping long enough to look around. Stacks of supplies with little space between them crowded the deck. Each stack had a man sitting or lying atop it. They differed in size, shape, and dress, but they shared one trait; each glared at him.

Sven walked toward the stern until he found a gangway and descended. He stood at the bottom of the ladder as his eyes adjusted to the dimness. To his left soldiers ate their evening meal. Lt. Castner stood with his back toward Sven.

As he ducked behind a support beam he heard the lieutenant say, "... think he is a stowaway. Watch for him."

Sven did not wait to hear more; he hurried into the darker interior. With each step he looked into another scowling face. His hope of finding a friendly miner with whom to journey from Skagway to Circle City faded.

Sven descended another gangway into the musty, hay-smelling blackness of the hold. He sat on the bottom rung of the ladder and ate a dry cheese sandwich from his duffel bag. He listened to the loud throbbing of steam-driven pistons as his eyes focused on an orange glow.

Feeling along what seemed to be a high board fence, Sven shuffled toward the glow. He inched his way to the open door of the ship's furnace room. A bare-backed muscular black man rhythmically shoveled coal into the fire box.

"Ouch." The word escaped Sven as he bumped his head.

"Who's dat?" The black man, ready to strike with

his shovel, whirled around. "Why's you sneakin' 'round here?"

"I'm your helper." Sven's quick wit helped again. "It's mealtime, Mister ... I forgot your name."

"Jefferson," the man answered as he stared at Sven. "You's small fer coal shovelin' ain't you, Boy? Da Cap'n say he'd find 'nother man."

Sven ignored the question. "Dinner time, Mister Jefferson. I'll shovel while you eat."

"You calls me Jefferson. Ever'body do. What's yo' name?"

"Sven."

"All right, skinny Sven, you's shovelin' en I's eatin'." Jefferson chuckled to himself and muttered, "Skinny Sven, skinny Sven."

"Bring me back some biscuits," Sven called after him. "Maybe I'll become fatter."

Sven's arms and back ached before Jefferson returned and looked into the furnace.

"You's doin' good, skinny Sven. Eat." He held out his bulging red kerchief.

Sven's eyes widened as he opened the bundle. "Thank you, Jefferson."

In addition to three biscuits, the kerchief held a baked potato and two slabs of ham. He ate greedily.

"I's dinkin' dat da cap'n not send you," Jefferson said and grinned. "You's stow'way."

Sven nodded. He had to stop telling lies.

Jefferson grinned. "I's dinkin' so. You helps me en I helps you. I's not tellin''bout stow'way. I'uz goin' t'ask 'bout you when da cap'n say he's not hire 'nother shoveler en ken I do da work alone? I says 'Yus, Sur,' 'cuse I knows you's here. You's ta shovel hard when da cap'n ring da signal bell. Dree bell mean you shovel mo' coal; two bell mean stop; fo' bell mean bank da fire. Ken you duz dat?"

"I can, Jefferson." Sven grinned back. He had a place to

hide until they reached Skagway. "Thanks for not telling."

"Dat's good," Jefferson said. "Now I's helpin' you hide. Take off yo' shirt." He scraped up handsful of coal dust and smeared them over Sven's body and face and into his blond hair.

"Dere, skinny Sven, you's lookin' like black man coal shoveler. I's callin' you skinny Sam." Jefferson chuckled and Sven laughed. Even his mother would not recognize him.

As the *Valencia* steamed north, Sven hid in the coal pile when anyone approached the furnace room. For a few minutes each night he sneaked on deck to breathe fresh ocean air. From the rail he stared at the shadowy wooded shoreline and snowcapped mountains and imagined how beautiful it might look in bright sunlight.

He never lingered. Jefferson waited for his turn on deck.

"We's gettin' ta Haines tomorrow," Jefferson said on their fifth night out from Seattle. "Ken you keeps a secret, Sam?"

"Sure," Sven replied.

"I's jumpin' ship in Haines en goin' ta Dawson ta find gold. Duz you wants ta go?"

"I want to get to Circle City to find my father," Sven said. "I thought we were going to Skagway."

"We's not goin' to Skagway. Ship's goin' to Valdez. I's gettin' off in Haines en findin' 'nother way ta Skagway."

"I'll go."

"Dat's good, Sam. We's needin' supplies. I'uz gettin' mine back ever' night. T'night you's gettin' some."

"How? Where?"

"You takes. Dere's supplies on deck. Men's sleepin'. We's needin' pots en fry pan. T'night you takes." Jefferson grinned.

"That's stealing." Sven's parents had taught him never to steal.

"Dat's so, but I has ta. Dree men beats me in Seattle en steals my supplies. Dat's when I's takin' job as fireman. I's takin' back 'nough ta gets ta Dawson, dat's all."

"I'll try." Sven agreed because Jefferson was helping him. "I never stole anything before."

On deck he glanced fearfully in every direction as he crept toward a stack of supplies. As he reached under a tarpaulin, a boot kicked him in the side. "Get away, nigger boy, or you'll get a knife in your back. We know your black daddy's been stealing. Tonight he'll jump overboard." The man laughed cruelly.

Sven stumbled toward the gangway but stopped. Two men, one tall and slender, the other shorter and heavier, leaned against a stack of boxes and looked out over the water. Sven recognized the tall man as Lt. Castner. He ducked into the shadows and listened.

"Lieutenant," the stocky man said, "we will be loading fifty reindeer when we are in Haines. They were shipped from Norway for our use as pack animals as we build a trail to the Yukon River. Our country's leaders don't believe Americans traveling to the gold fields should need to go through Canada. In the morning I want you to help me make arrangements to load the reindeer."

"Yes, Sir, Captain Glenn. Orders are orders, and I am determined to reach Circle City. I will be ready."

Circle City, that's where I am going, Sven thought as he crawled to the gangway and backed down the ladder.

"You's back fast. Wat you gets?" Jefferson asked as Sven entered the furnace room.

"A kick in the ribs. They're waiting for you, Jefferson. They know you've been stealing and plan to throw you overboard. Don't go."

"You's not ta be worryin', skinny Sam." Jefferson grinned and pulled a big knife from his boot top. "I's takin' care."

Sven shoveled coal and prayed as he waited for Jefferson to return.

2

"I tell you, Captain Adams, there's a young one. If we didn't need a fireman to get to Skagway, the two of them would have jumped overboard."

Sven leaped into the coal bin when he heard the harsh voice. From behind the coal pile he watched Lt. Castner and two other men enter the furnace room.

"That's strange. There's no one here," the gray haired, stocky ship's captain said.

"Are you sure he was a Negro?" Lt. Castner asked. "Like I told Captain Adams, first evening out I found a boy hiding on deck. He disappeared and I haven't seen him since."

"You must be blind, Lieutenant. He crawled past you after I kicked him. Then his daddy, the one I saw stealing, came up. When he saw us he jumped overboard."

"With your and your friends' knives prodding him," Lt. Castner said. "I know what I saw."

Sven bit his lip when he heard, and tears welled up in his eyes. He wished Jefferson had listened to him.

"That's done, Gentlemen. I'm captain here. If Jefferson sneaked his son aboard and was stealing, he deserved what he got. I hired one fireman, and someone stoked this fire all night, every time I rang the bell." The ship's captain peered into the dark coal bin. "Come out of there."

Sven hesitated and prayed. He brushed tears from each cheek as he stood up.

"There he is, like I said." The man who had kicked Sven pointed over the captain's shoulder. "Come here, nigger boy."

The three men stared as Sven, black from hair to heel, stepped from the coal bin.

"What's your name?"

"His name is Sven Johanson, Captain," Lt. Castner said. "I never saw a Negro with blue eyes like his, nor one whose tears washed the black away." He reached down and pulled up Sven's trouser leg. "Certainly not one with white legs."

"B'gory. I'll be a bowlegged monkey. A white boy trying to be black. Bet he's the one I saw stealing our first day out from Seattle," the rib-kicker said.

"I never stole anything," Sven said. "I was hiding from Lieutenant Castner."

"That is true," Lt. Castner said. "I accidentally discovered his hiding place. We talked and then he disappeared."

"How about it, Boy? Sven is it?" Capt. Adams asked. "Is that true?"

"Yes, Sir." Sven told the captain how Jefferson helped him and more tears welled up in his eyes.

"Are you crying for Jefferson?" Lt. Castner asked.

"Yes, Sir. He was kind to me, and now he's dead." Sven stifled a sob.

"I'm not so sure he drowned. I saw him swimming."

The rib-kicker laughed cruelly. "He'd never make it. The water is too cold."

"Forget Jefferson. I need a fireman until we dock in Haines," Capt. Adams said. "I'll call that your fare. After that you are on your own. How old are you?"

"Eighteen," Sven lied. His blackened face hid the red flush of his cheeks as Lt. Castner stared at him.

"You sure are puny," the captain said. "If you had more muscle I would hire you until we arrive back in Seattle."

"Captain," Lt. Castner said, "don't forget that we have exploring to do after we leave Haines."

"I know, Valdez and Prince William Sound. Good old Uncle Sam will pay me well for that. Get to work, Sven."

"B'gory," the rib-kicking miner swore. "Ain't we going to Skagway?"

"No," Capt. Adams said, "the army hired this boat. You may find another way to Skagway or stay on board to Valdez."

"B'gory. There'll be trouble when the men hear this." The miner stamped from the boiler room.

"Don't worry, Captain," Lt. Castner said, "the army is on your side. Sven, you can turn around at Haines and head for home."

Sven stoked the furnace until early afternoon when the *Valencia* docked. He watched from the rail as twelve miners unloaded supplies. The others stayed on the ship. He watched Lt. Castner, with Capt. Glenn and six more soldiers, walk down the gangplank.

"Are you Sven?" a smiling black-haired soldier asked him.

"Yes, Sir."

"Off you go. Lieutenant Castner asked me to give you this, and to tell you to return home. 'Alaska's no place for a boy by himself,' the lieutenant said. Get yourself a place for sleep and a bath, and food, and catch the first ship to Seattle. Lieutenant said there should be enough money." He handed Sven a small leather pouch, pulled shut and wrapped around with a long drawstring.

"Thank you, and thank Lieutenant Castner," Sven said and walked down the gangplank. He stopped on the dock and peered at the coins in the pouch. He walked into Haines and looked for a place to sleep and, especially, for a place to take a bath.

"Eke! Get out!" a woman screamed as he stepped through her door.

Sven stepped backward. "Your sign says 'Room, Board, and Bath.' I need all three."

"The bath first. In the shed out back. You are the dirtiest young man that ever stepped through my door."

Sven ran around the boarding house to a small shed. A metal stove had water heating on it. A wooden tub stood on the floor.

The woman stuck her head in a window. "Use all the water you need. Do you have clean clothes?"

Sven nodded.

"Good. Then scrub those you are wearing. Don't want that dirt in my house. Come in for dinner when you are clean."

"Thank you, Ma'am." Sven stripped and scrubbed until he felt clean enough to enter the house.

———

After a comfortable night's sleep in a bed and a hearty breakfast, Sven walked toward the dock. He had a new plan for finding his father. Since Lt. Castner was determined to reach Circle City, somehow, he would go with the lieutenant.

Sven waited in the mist near the dock. His hope for reboarding the *Valencia* depended on his disguise. He wore two pair of canvas trousers, his sweater and two plaid shirts under his Mackinaw. His food filled duffel bag under his shirts provided a large lumpy stomach. His slicker covered his odd heavy shape. Soot from the boarding house fireplace, dabbed unto his cheeks and chin, was meant to look like a stubbly beard. With collar up and knit cap pulled down, he might look like an old man.

The first test of Sven's disguise came as the sun, rising over the mountains, filtered through the mist. Lt. Castner and another officer walked past inches from where he sat on a barrel.

"It's a waste of time," the other officer said. "Those reindeer will not be any healthier tomorrow than they were yesterday."

"We need them for pack animals, Lowe," Lt. Castner said. "We only have sick mules coming from Dyea."

"Sick mules, sick reindeer," Lowe said. "We all will be carrying our own packs."

Sven sighed with relief. Lt. Castner had only glanced at him.

He watched a small ship edge toward the dock. On its deck stood several mules and five horses. As a gangplank was lowered from its deck, a dock level hatch was opened into the hold of the *Valencia*.

A civilian and four soldiers began leading the animals toward the gangplank.

"Stupid mules, move," one of the soldiers said and swore. "Dillon, I need some help."

"Got my hands full," the civilian replied. He led two mules down the gangplank.

Sven ran toward the small ship. His success with mules on the family farm when they lived in Minnesota could be useful. He hurried to the deck.

In a deep, rough voice, Sven said, "Here, Soldier, let me help. I'm good with animals." He grabbed the lead ropes of the stubborn mules.

"Come on, mules," he spoke softly into the mules' ears and rubbed their noses. "Let's go. Come now." He backed down the gangplank with the mules following. On the dock he took a lead rope in each hand and, still talking, led the mules into the *Valencia*.

With the large hatch open, Sven saw what he had not seen before. What felt like fences were stalls for mules, horses, and reindeer, and a large pile of hay. He followed Dillon into a stall and handed him the lead ropes.

"I'll get hay," Sven said gruffly.

He forked hay into the feed racks before the horses and mules. As he did he dug a hole into the side of the hay pile. With no one watching, he pulled hay down over the hole and burrowed into his snug hiding place. He removed his slicker and a layer of clothes before lying down.

Loud talking awakened Sven.

"Close the hatch. We can't wait any longer."

"The Norwegians agreed to have the reindeer here."

"We will go without them. The tide is going out and we sail with the tide. Close the hatch."

"Drat it all." The hatch banged shut. "Now all we have for pack animals are sick mules and horses."

Sven smiled as he listened to the familiar throb of the engine and felt the *Valencia* move. He stretched his legs and felt for a biscuit in his duffel bag.

3

Sven lay beneath the hay and listened. When all was quiet he crawled out. A lantern, hanging from a beam, dimly lit the hold. He crept to the foot of the gangway.

He breathed deeply. Air currents from above provided relief from the smelly, stagnant air in the hold.

For three days Sven stayed near the gangway to enjoy the fresher air. Each time Dillon and two soldiers tended the animals, forking hay or shoveling manure, he burrowed deep into his hiding place. Twice he hid in the mules' stall to avoid discovery by the new fireman.

When the *Valencia* docked, Sven listened beneath the gangway. He heard nothing. Curious, he inched his way up and poked his head out to scan the lower deck. Empty.

He walked to a dirty porthole and peered out. A few small houses and two larger buildings formed a small village. A smaller ship was tied to the opposite side of the dock. Between the ships stood five men. Sven recognized captains Adams and Glenn.

He dropped to his knees and sprawled into a shadow when a noise startled him. As soldiers descended from the top deck, he crouched behind a pile of miners' supplies and watched. He counted as Lt. Castner and twenty-seven other soldiers lined up.

"'Tention," Lt. Castner ordered as Capt. Glenn descended the gangway.

"At ease," Capt. Glenn ordered. "Lieutenant Learnard, have your squad prepare to move aboard the *Salmo*. You, your men, and I will begin searching for a pass through the Chugach Mountains.

"Lieutenant Castner, you and your squad stay on the *Valencia*. After Captain Abercrombie and his company unload at Valdez, continue westward and look for an ice free harbor. It will serve as our base for inland exploration. Do you understand?"

Lt. Castner's heels clicked together and he stood taller and straighter than usual as he snapped to attention. "Yes, Sir."

"One more thing. After you establish camp, use the *Valencia* and search for a starting point for a trail into the interior."

"Yes, Sir."

From his hiding place Sven watched as half the soldiers packed their duffel bags. He sighed with relief as all the soldiers returned to the upper deck. He quickly descended into the hold and the safety of the hay.

He prayed and thought about Lt. Castner. The stiff, cold lieutenant had provided money for his return to Seattle. How would the lieutenant react to finding him on the *Valencia* again?

He burrowed deeper into the hay and dozed.

Sven awakened as the ship shuddered to a rocking stop. Shouts and stamping feet sounded over his head. He crawled from the hay and saw the fireman climbing the gangway. He listened until the noise overhead died away.

He had climbed halfway up the ladder when he heard steps. He jumped down and crouched in the shadows. Soldiers stepped inches above his head as they descended into the hold.

They opened the side hatch and Sven looked out. Miners in small boats loaded with gear rowed toward shore. On the beach other miners gathered around growing stacks of supplies. Tied against the *Valencia* was a flat barge.

"Half of the mules and three horses."

The voice attracted Sven. He looked at the men who had entered the stalls and recognized Lt. Castner and Dillon, the civilian mule handler.

Under Dillon's supervision the soldiers blindfolded the mules and horses and led them onto the barge. After an officer and the soldiers stepped onto the barge, Lt. Castner and Dillon closed the hatch.

"That leaves only us and the ship's crew, Dillon," Lt. Castner said as the two men climbed the gangway.

And me. Sven smiled as he thought of how surprised Lt. Castner would be.

———

The bell rang three times. Sven waited, but the fireman did not return. After several minutes Capt. Adams and Lt. Castner descended the gangway.

"No, I don't know," Capt. Adams said. "Maybe he's asleep."

The two men entered the furnace room.

"Rats! Not again!"

Sven heard the captain's loud exclamation.

"That no good fireman jumped ship. What do I do now?" Angry, Capt. Adams stomped from the furnace room.

"Calm down, Captain," Lt. Castner said. "I'll assign my men to take turns as firemen."

"They won't know the bell signals."

Sven stepped from the shadows under the gangway. "I know the signals."

"Sven?" Lt. Castner gasped. "I thought you returned to Seattle."

"I'm going to Circle City, Sir," Sven said.

"How did you get back on board? I had soldiers watching the gangplank."

Sven grinned. "I helped lead mules aboard. I'm good with animals."

"We should send you ashore," Lt. Castner said, but he did not sound angry. "What do you say, Captain?"

"We should," Capt. Adams agreed, "but I need a fireman. Sven knows what to do and he knows the signals. Fire up, Sven. You're my fireman again."

"Only until I leave for Circle City," Sven muttered as he hurried to the furnace room.

Shoveling hard, he built the fire to raise steam pressure in the boiler. He smiled. The monotonous, tiring work gave him a reason for being on the *Valencia*. Hard work would not hurt him, and, best of all, he was helping to move the ship forward, closer to finding his father.

———

That evening, with the ship anchored, Sven rested on deck. Icebergs, calved from tidewater glaciers, floated in the frigid waters. Snowcapped mountains and lush green islands circled the horizon. He sucked in fresh cool air and wondered how he would become the next fireman to jump ship.

"You, Sven," the friendly black-haired soldier said, "I thought I sent you home to Seattle."

Sven smiled at the soldier who had given him Lt. Castner's money. "You did, but I am going to Circle City to join my father."

"My name's Hugh McGregor, call me Mac," the soldier said and held out his hand. "How are you going there?"

Sven shook the soldier's hand and answered, "With you."

"Does Lieutenant Castner know this?" McGregor asked.

"Not yet," Sven answered and smiled. "Not yet."

With his dark eyes McGregor studied Sven's face. "Hmm. You got this far. How old are you?"

"Eighteen."

"Eighteen? I don't believe it. How old are you really?"

Sven felt his face redden as McGregor stared into his eyes. He dropped his head. Tired of lying, he whispered, "Promise not to tell?"

"I promise. How old are you?"

"Fourteen."

"You're a brave one, rushing off for gold by yourself." McGregor patted Sven on the shoulder. "Your secret is safe with me."

"I really am going to join my father."

"Really? I thought you were a runaway. Why else would you stowaway?"

"You have to believe me, Mac. I want to find my father."

McGregor smiled. "That must be the truth, Sven. You blush when you lie. But don't worry, I won't tell."

"Thanks, Mac." Sven turned and descended the gang-way, and hoped he could trust McGregor.

During daylight hours the next two days, Sven shoveled coal. Capt. Adams guided the *Valencia* into several inlets as Lt. Castner searched for a campsite. The afternoon of the third day the search ended at the head of Portage Bay. Sven relaxed when the bell signaled him to bank the fire.

His chore completed, he hurried to the deck.

"Over here, Sven," McGregor called him to the rail and pointed.

Sven saw Lt. Castner and two soldiers rowing a small boat toward a cluster of tents on the beach. "Where are they going?"

"To find a campsite."

"Does that mean we'll leave the ship soon?" Sven asked.

"No, we must find a way through the mountains first and we need to wait for Captain Glenn."

Sven smiled; he had time to plan. He relaxed with the soldiers on deck as they watched sea birds soaring along the shore and sea otters frolicking near the stern of the ship.

When Lt. Castner returned he said, "We'll set up camp there." He pointed toward a grove of spruce trees a mile from the miners' camp. "Notice how the wind has shaped the trees. We'll set our tents in the lee of those trees?"

"In the snow, Sir?" one soldier asked as they stared toward the spruce grove. Though it was late April, the drifts of winter snow had not melted.

"In the snow, Van," Lt. Castner answered. "Dig down. It will help shelter the tents. There's a stream for water. Mac, Powers, when we get ashore you cut firewood. There are dead trees in the grove."

"May I go ashore, Sir?" Sven asked.

"You work for Captain Adams. Ask him."

Sven turned toward the captain.

"Not today, Sven," Capt. Adams said. "Maybe another day. Now would be a good afternoon for you to shovel coal nearer to the furnace. You rested long enough."

"Yes, Sir." Sven returned to the furnace room. As he shoveled he wondered how and when he would get off the *Valencia*, and if the lieutenant would ever stop being so soldierly stiff and formal. If he could not make friends with Lieutenant Castner, he might never reach Circle City.

4

MOST mornings for the next three weeks Sven fired the furnace. Lt. Castner directed Capt. Adams into inlet and bay in search of a trail across the Chugach Mountains.

When the bell signaled for Sven to bank the fire, he smothered the flames with ashes. With that finished he rushed to the deck. Each day he hoped Lt. Castner would allow him to join the explorers.

"May I come ashore this time, Sir?" Sven asked.

Lt. Castner's answer remained the same. "You are the ship's fireman. You work for Captain Adams."

Sven watched as Lt. Castner, with five or six of his men, rowed a small boat to a beach or the mouth of a stream. With Capt. Adams' binoculars he scanned rocky cliffs and calving glaciers. He watched seals sitting on icebergs and sea lions sunning on rocks. Occasionally he spotted bald eagles perched on tree tops near water's edge. One day he watched a pod of orcas, the tall-finned black and white killer whales, circle the ship.

Mostly he watched the progress of Lt. Castner and his men. They seldom stayed on shore long. Their efforts failed as cliffs or waterfalls blocked their advances. Twice Sven watched as they scrambled to escape tons of snow and rock plummeting down narrow valleys.

"An avalanche will kill them all," Capt. Adams

predicted, but every soldier returned after each exploring excursion.

"Go stoke the fire," Capt. Adams said each time the men began rowing back toward the ship.

"Yes, Sir," Sven answered.

That became a game for Sven. When the captain said "Go ..." he said "Yes, Sir," and dashed for the gangway. He tried to reach the ladder before the captain finished saying "...stoke the fire."

Most nights the *Valencia* returned to the camp on Portage Bay. A few nights they remained anchored in other inlets. It did not matter to Sven. He slept in the hay which provided a softer bed than the wooden bunks in the crew's cabin. He became friends with the mules and horses and was close to the furnace room. When the bell rang in the morning he awoke and stoked the fire.

———

One morning during the second week of fruitless searching, Sven banked the fire and hurried to the deck.

Lt. Castner had six men picked for the first exploring party of the day. "We have had no success finding any way to cross the mountains so far. Today," he said and pointed, "we will try to cross that glacier."

"May I go?" Sven asked.

"You're the ship's fireman," Lt. Castner said and smiled at Sven's persistence. "Let's go, men."

Sven propped his arms on the deck rail to steady the binoculars. He watched the seven men row to shore and hike up the hillside along the glacier to its top. He watched as they walked across it.

"Ah," Sven gasped as one soldier suddenly disappeared in a fluff of snow. "Captain, one of the men fell."

Capt. Adams took the binoculars and watched the men on the glacier.

"What are they doing?" Sven asked.

"Can't see. Looks like they have a rope. Somebody maybe fell into a crevasse. I always expected someone to get killed."

"Let me look." Sven reached for the binoculars.

"They're pulling him up with the rope, Captain. He's out. They're carrying him. They're coming back."

"Go ..."

"Yes, Sir." Sven handed the binoculars to Capt. Adams and raced for the gangway.

"... stoke up the fire."

Sven had the steam up in the boiler and waited on deck when the rowboat returned. McGregor and Powers helped bruised and scratched Private Woodruff up a ladder and to a bunk on the second deck.

"Take us back to camp, Captain," Lt. Castner ordered. "No more glaciers. Woodruff had a close call."

Sven hurried to the furnace room.

———

Back in Portage Bay that evening Capt. Adams stopped Sven as he started down the gangway. "Sven."

"Yes, Sir."

"Sleep late. Lieutenant Castner says we will stay in camp tomorrow for a day of rest. Time for camp chores, laundry, haircuts, he says."

"May I go ashore?"

"We'll see, Sven. I don't know why not."

"Thank you, Sir, and good night." He had not been on land since the ship left Haines.

———

"Still want to go ashore?" Capt. Adams asked in the morning.

"Yes, Sir. I have laundry to do."

"Get your things. We'll go soon."

Sven hurried to the hold. He stuffed everything he owned into his duffel bag and raced up the gangway.

When the rowboat reached shore Sven ran toward the soldiers' camp. "Mac," he called as looked for his friend.

"He's at the river doing laundry, Sven," Pvt. Powers said and pointed toward a trail.

Sven hiked through the trees to where several soldiers laundered clothes in the cold water. He watched as some rubbed bar soap into dirty shirts and trousers, others swished clothing in the stream.

"Sven," McGregor called when he saw him, "got some laundry?"

"Yes, Sir, Mac." He dumped everything out of his duffel bag.

"You going to wash that?" McGregor pointed to his wool Mackintosh coat.

"No, but I have a plan. I need your help." Sven stuffed the Mackintosh, extra shoes, sweater, and his slicker back into the bag. "May I use your soap?"

Mac handed Sven the bar of soap. "How can I help?"

"Will you keep my duffel bag until I jump ship?"

"So, are you planning to do that? Why don't you go home? Circle City is a long way."

"Mac, you know I'm going to join my father."

"Do you have brothers or sisters?"

"Two sisters and a brother."

"Are you the oldest?" McGregor questioned.

"Yes."

"Why don't you go back and help your mother? With your father gone she needs you."

"She wants me to find my father." Sven scrubbed harder and kept his head down as he felt the rush of warm blood redden his cheeks.

"So, another lie?" McGregor asked.

"Will you help me?"

"Only if you tell the truth."

Sven remained quiet as he scrubbed and rinsed his clothes. He felt McGregor's dark eyes watching as he draped his wet clothing over alder branches.

"Would you like to catch a fish, Sven?" McGregor asked

and smiled. He held up string, hooks, and a piece of meat.

"Sure."

"Come along."

McGregor led the way upstream to where a large tree had toppled down at a bend in the river. He climbed out on the tree and sat down.

"Sit. I caught three trout under here." He cut two long lengths of string, tied hooks on them, and baited them with meat.

"Tie the end around your hand," he said as he handed one string to Sven.

"So, Sven," McGregor said as they dangled their lines in the river, "tell me the truth and I will help you."

Sven looked at McGregor. Mac had kept his word and not told anyone that he was fourteen and not eighteen. "Promise?"

"Yes."

"And you won't tell anyone else?"

McGregor nodded.

"My father left for the Klondike in August of ninety-six, two years ago," Sven said, "when the first stories of gold were in the newspaper. Last July we received a letter that he wrote in Circle City in March. He said he would be home before Christmas.

"He didn't come and mother worried that something happened to him. Every night I heard her crying. She said she knew he was dead and she talked about going back to our old home in Minnesota.

"'Mother,' I would say, 'if we move away, father won't be able to find us. Let me go to Alaska to find him.'"

"So, he didn't ask for you to join him, Sven?"

"No, Mac, but I have to. I know he is alive."

"And you ran away?"

"Yes, I had to. Mother planned to sell our house and return to Minnesota. I have to tell my father."

Tears welled up in Sven's eyes as he thought about leaving his mother. He did not tell McGregor how he ran away at the last possible time. Their house had been sold.

He handed his oldest sister a note for his mother and hid in the crowd as the rest of the family boarded a train for Minnesota. He had not said goodbye.

McGregor patted Sven's shoulder. "I'll help you, but I really think you should return home. Your mother will need you if your father does not return."

"I intend to return home right after I find my father. We'll return home together."

"Will you make a promise to me?" McGregor asked.

"What?"

"If you do not find your father in Circle City, will you stop searching and go home?"

Sven closed his eyes in thought. "What if I learn where he is?"

"Then you may go to him; if not you go home. Promise?"

"I promise." Sven sighed. He felt relieved for having told, and for having Mac as a friend.

"Good. Now let's catch some fish."

Sven smiled at Mac and jiggled his line.

5

EIGHT days later, as the *Valencia* anchored in Portage Bay, Sven heard Lt. Castner say, "Captain Adams, our quest is hopeless. We cannot find a pass through the mountains. We will stay in camp tomorrow."

"Whatever you say," Capt. Adams said and laughed. "Uncle Sam pays me the same every day."

"Sven?"

"Yes, Sir?"

"Do you think you could catch a few more fish tomorrow? Those you caught last week tasted delicious."

"Oh, yes, Sir." Morning could not come soon enough.

———

"Captain Adams wants me to catch more fish, Mac," Sven said when he found his friend the next morning. "May you go?"

"The lieutenant gave us the day off. Wait here." McGregor fetched his string and hooks, and bacon from the camp kitchen. "So, ready to catch a big one?"

"Ready." Sven followed McGregor to their fishing tree.

———

The loud blast of a ship's steam whistle ended their fishing.

"What's that, Mac. It's not the *Valencia.*"

"Maybe it's the *Salmo,*" McGregor said. "Lieutenant Castner expects Captain Glenn. Let's go see."

They trotted back to camp. As McGregor greeted his friends from the *Salmo,* Sven looked for Lt. Castner and Capt. Glenn. As he walked near Lt. Castner's tent he heard their voices. He crept close and listened.

"... no trail, Captain," he heard Lt. Castner say.

"I agree. We found nothing either. Did you know I sent Lieutenant Learnard across Portage Glacier to look for a pass from Turnagain Arm? He has not returned."

"So what now, Sir?"

"Well, Lieutenant, I want you to cross too. We have wasted enough time here."

"Yes, Sir."

"Leave tomorrow. Ask the miners you meet if they know a way into the interior. Hire one to be our guide."

Tomorrow, Sven thought. I have to jump ship today. He walked toward the woods.

"Sven, where are you going?" McGregor called after him.

"To fish. I promised Captain Adams fish for dinner." He felt his face redden, but McGregor could not see it.

"Good luck."

"Thanks." He would need good luck. He ducked off the trail into a dense thicket.

———

Only a sliver moon and bright stars aided Sven that night as he sneaked back into camp.

He crept into McGregor's tent and whispered in his ear, "Mac, wake up. I need my duffel bag."

"Huh? What?"

"Ssh. Mac, it's me, Sven. Tonight's the night. I jumped ship so I can follow Lieutenant Castner tomorrow. Where's my duffel bag?"

"So, that's why Captain Adams couldn't find you and you weren't fishing?"

"Yes. Where's my bag?"

"Are you sure you want to do this?"

"Yes, Mac. My bag?"

"Under my cot. Good luck."

"Thanks." Sven pulled the bag from its hiding place and crawled from the tent.

He walked in shadows toward the miners' camp before hiding to wait for Lt. Castner.

———

In the gray early dawn Sven followed Lt. Castner. The lieutenant joined four miners who drank coffee around a campfire. One man stood up.

Sven watched as the man squirmed into his pack and led Lt. Castner toward Portage Glacier. When the two disappeared from view he ran toward the fire. He stopped and puffed as if he had run a long way. "Lieutenant Castner ... Where is he? ... I was supposed to go ..."

"Calm down, Boy," a gray-bearded man said. "Catch your breath."

"You're too late," said a man in a plaid shirt.

"Which way?" Sven asked.

"You can't cross the glacier by yourself," the old man said. "You need to know the trail."

"Are you going across?" Sven asked.

"Later, when it is light enough to see."

"May I go with you?"

"We don't need a boy along," plaid shirt said. "Go back to the soldiers."

"I can make it," Sven argued. "I can take care of myself."

"I say let him come," the old man said. "He needs to join his lieutenant. What do you say, Jake?"

Jake, the third man, squinted at Sven. "Follow us. I don't care. If you get into trouble, that's your problem."

"I won't get into trouble."

Sven waited impatiently as the three men packed their supplies. Each loaded a heavy pack onto his back. Sven flipped his small duffel bag over his shoulder and followed.

"Watch out for crevasses," the old man said as they began crossing the glacier.

Sven nodded and followed the silent men. He concentrated on his footing. The trail became increasingly slippery as the top layer of ice and snow softened. It became treacherous as wind-driven rain blew into their faces as they neared the Turnagain Arm of Cook Inlet.

Sven pulled his slicker from his duffel bag and wondered what he should do. He had no tent, and he hoped to wait longer before surprising Lt. Castner for a third time.

———

"That's Spruce Camp ahead." The old man pointed as they sloshed through the slush of the glacier's tongue.

Sven looked at tents scattered among the trees. "Thanks for letting me join you. I hope I find my lieutenant. He has the tent."

"Boy," the old man said, "help set up my tent and stay with me until you find your lieutenant."

Sven looked at plaid shirt and Jake.

"Don't mind them," the old man said. "We joined up to hike over the glacier. Help me and have a place to stay dry."

"Thank you, Sir. I'll do it."

"Not sir. Call me Tunis, Tunis VanderWerff." He held out his hand. "What's your name?"

"Sven, Sven Olafsen." He did not need to lie to the old man.

He helped set up the tent and gathered firewood. Tunis built a smoky fire beneath the branches of a spruce tree.

"Stack the wood under the tree, near the fire, Sven, so it will dry. Then go look for your lieutenant. Come back when you're hungry."

Head down against the wind and rain, Sven cautiously walked from tent to tent. He hid behind trees when he saw anyone out in the wet weather. When he did not see Lt. Castner, he returned to Tunis and a meal of beans and coffee.

"Find your lieutenant, Sven?"

"No, all the tents look the same and everyone is inside."

"Can't go anywhere in this weather," Tunis said. "Stay with me. If you don't find your lieutenant you can be my partner. I can use a strong young man like you."

"Thank you, Tunis, but no thanks. I am going with the army to Circle City, to join my father."

———

For two days, until the wind blew clouds and rain away, Sven stayed with Tunis. He frequently walked among the tents to look for Lt. Castner.

Sven ducked behind a tent when he saw him talking with another lieutenant.

"You're sure there is no way through the mountains?" Lt. Castner asked as he stroked his chin.

"No, none. I'm going to report to Captain Glenn. If this good weather holds, I'll cross the glacier in the morning," the other officer said.

"Tell him I've gone across Turnagain Arm to Sunrise City. I'm leaving as soon as I pack."

Sven turned his back on the two officers and hurried to Tunis' tent.

"I've found Lieutenant Castner. He wants to leave for Sunrise City right away," Sven said as he took his duffel bag from the tent. "Thanks, Tunis, thanks for everything."

He pulled the small pouch from beneath his shirt and handed a coin to the old man. "Take this for the food." He placed one of Lt. Castner's coins in Tunis' palm as they shook hands. "Goodbye."

Keeping out of sight, he hurried toward the lieutenants' tent. The other lieutenant watched Lt. Castner depart. Moving stealthily from tree to tree, Sven followed.

Lt. Castner took long strides and Sven lagged far

behind as they hiked the narrow trail around the east end of Turnagain Arm.

———

Sven stared in surprise when he saw Quartz Camp; there were more tents than he could count. But his doubts of finding the lieutenant soon vanished. He joined a group of men who listened as Lt. Castner related news about a possible war with Spain over conditions in Cuba.

"I asked for a transfer to a fighting unit," Lt. Castner said, "but I don't think I will get it. I am here with an army company to develop a trail to Circle City on the Yukon River. By fall you should be able to walk there from here."

Some of the listeners laughed at his prediction, but others asked questions about the expedition.

After Lt. Castner answered the miners' questions, he asked, "How do I get to Sunrise City?"

"I'll take you, Lieutenant," a muscular young miner said. "I planned to go there anyway. We'll go at high tide tomorrow."

"High tide?" Lt. Castner questioned.

"I have a boat," the man said. "I am not going to pack all my supplies. It's a long hike."

Sven turned away as the cluster of men broke up. "How far is it to Sunrise City?" he asked the nearest miner.

"About twenty-five miles."

"Where is the trail?"

"Can't miss it," the man said. "Starts beyond the last tent." He pointed down the long row of tents.

"Thanks." Sven shifted his duffel bag to his other shoulder. In the lengthening daylight of the Alaska spring he could hike until late.

6

SVEN hiked steadily on the well-worn trail until it ended at a wide stream. He looked right, then left; no trail. He saw it across the stream. With shoes and stockings stuffed in his duffel bag and trouser legs rolled high, he stepped into the frigid water. One step, two steps, three; he grimaced. The rocks hurt his feet and banged his ankles each time he slipped.

"Ow. This won't work," he said to himself and returned to the bank.

With shoes on his bare feet he waded in. At midstream the water pushed against his thighs, and he leaned into the current to keep his footing. He shivered and shuffled forward. Safely across he sat and rested; he dried his legs and feet with his extra shirt.

Crossing streams became routine: wade across, dry off, take a drink, relax. In a warm, sunny resting place he fell asleep.

———

The sun hung low in the sky when Sven awakened. He shook his head and stretched. His movement startled a large moose that stood by the stream. The turn of the moose's head alerted Sven to its presence.

"It's all right, moose," Sven said softly. "Go ahead, take a drink. I won't hurt you."

The moose cocked its ears forward and listened. Sven talked softly as he backed away. He had not thought about the danger of hiking alone, unarmed, through the Alaska wilderness. He prayed for safety, and sang and talked as he hurried along the trail.

As twilight deepened, Sven climbed into a spruce tree. The needles scratched and pulled at his clothes, but, sitting ten feet up on a sturdy branch, he felt safe. He listened to the night sounds: an owl hooting, small animals scurrying beneath his tree, the distant howling of wolves. As his eyes adjusted to the dim light, he watched a snowshoe hare nibbling grass beneath his perch.

As dawn brightened the sky, Sven climbed down and resumed his hike. His stomach growled, reminding him that he had eaten nothing since yesterday's breakfast. He wondered how much farther it was to Sunrise City.

The sun stood high over the mountains when he spotted a tent in the trees. "Anyone there?" he called.

A head wearing a weather-beaten hat popped up from behind the tent. "What do you want?"

"How far to Sunrise City?"

"You're there," the man said. "Just stay on the trail."

"Where can I buy breakfast?"

"Johnson's Store. Straight ahead."

"Thank you." Sven waved and walked on.

He saw more tents in the trees along the trail, and small cabins. The trail widened into a street with cabins on both sides. He read Johnson's on the front of a building and walked in. Three empty tables stood near the front window.

"What do you need?" a gruff male voice asked as Sven sat down.

"Breakfast."

"You got money?"

"Some. How much is breakfast?"

"Hot cakes, bacon, fried 'taters, and coffee; two dollars or a pinch of gold dust. Hot cakes, all you can eat, and coffee; one dollar."

"Hot cakes and coffee," Sven ordered. He watched men on the street as he waited for his meal.

"Here's your cakes." The soft woman's voice surprised Sven.

He snapped his head around and looked into the face of the waitress, the first woman he had seen since leaving the boarding house in Haines. Her blue eyes, chubby cheeks, and kind smile reminded him of his mother.

"Never saw a woman before?"

"Not since I left Haines." A tear trickled down his cheek.

"Homesick?" the woman asked.

"A little."

"Then I will act like your mother." The woman smiled. "Quit dawdling and eat your breakfast."

Sven ate greedily.

"Slow down and enjoy your food. Yell for Emma when you need more cakes. Help yourself to coffee."

After gobbling down the first stack of hot cakes, Sven called Emma. He ate the second stack more slowly and called again.

Emma sat down at the table when she brought the third stack of cakes.

"When's the last time you ate?"

"Yesterday breakfast."

"Where at?"

"Spruce Camp." Sven answered between bites.

"Spruce Camp? You walked a long way on an empty stomach. What's your name?"

"Sven Olafsen."

"How old are you?"

"Fourteen. Fifteen in September."

"Are you a runaway?"

Sven nodded and told Emma how he had left his mother, sisters, and brother, to find his father in Circle City.

"How are you going to Circle City?" she asked. "It's a long walk. You're too young to go by yourself."

"With the army."

"I haven't seen any soldiers around here," Emma said.

"Lieutenant Castner is coming today, by boat."

"By boat? Are you sure?"

"He is coming from Quartz Camp with another man."

"Oh, a small boat," Emma said and laughed. "I was thinking of a ship. They only go to Hope." She frowned. "Why did he make you walk?"

Sven ignored her question. "Where's Hope?"

"Twelve miles down the trail." She looked at Sven's empty plate. "Had enough?"

"Plenty." Sven rubbed his full stomach. "And I'd like to buy some biscuits and jerky, too."

When he paid, Emma whispered in his ear, "Come in tomorrow morning, Sven. I'll pay for your hot cakes." She squeezed him with a half hug like his mother did.

Tears welled up in Sven's eyes as he walked toward the waterfront to watch for Lt. Castner's arrival. He found a sunny spot on a grassy slope near the pier. He lay back and, thinking of mother and home, fell asleep.

———

"Take my hand, Lieutenant."

The loud voice awakened Sven. He looked toward the pier where the miner from Quartz Camp gripped Lt. Castner's hand and pulled him from a rowboat.

"That wasn't so bad, now, was it?" the man said and grinned. "I told you we would make it."

"Not so bad, Oscar, not so bad, but I don't believe I would do it again." Lt. Castner smiled weakly as he hoisted his pack up from the pier.

Oscar grinned. "I'm sorry you feel that way. I hoped you would enjoy the adventure."

"Goodbye, Oscar." Walking unsteadily, Lt. Castner left Oscar on the pier.

Sven, staying where he could see without being seen, shadowed Lt. Castner. He watched as the lieutenant stopped to talk with every miner he met. He watched and ate biscuits and jerky as Lt. Castner dined with four miners in Johnson's Store. He wondered if Emma talked about him with the lieutenant.

That evening, when he saw the light go out in the cabin Lt. Castner had entered with another man, he donned his Mackintosh and curled up under his slicker.

———

Sven awakened when the sun's rays warmed him. He worried that Lt. Castner might have left. As his stomach growled he remembered Emma's promise of a free breakfast. I'll eat first and find the lieutenant later, he decided.

But Lt. Castner and another man sat at a table by the window of Johnson's store. Sven waited until they left before he entered.

"What do you want today?" the gruff voice sounded from the back.

"Hot cakes."

"Hot cakes for the boy, Emma."

"Good morning, Sven. Are you hungry again?" Emma asked when she served his food. "I brought you some bacon, too. Why didn't you eat with your lieutenant?"

"He said I could sleep late." Sven felt his face redden.

"Did you see him yesterday? He said he didn't know Sven Olafsen. He knows Sven Johanson. Is that you?"

Sven chewed hard and washed the food down with coffee as he thought of his answer. "I lied to the lieutenant when I joined the army in Haines. I joined to get to Circle City. I lied about my age too. When I find my father, I will be able to get out of the army because I lied."

Emma tousled his tangled blonde hair. "You are a smart boy. I'll get you more hot cakes. Then you will need to hurry. I heard the lieutenant say he will hike to Hope today. You don't want to keep him waiting."

Sven wolfed down his food. He returned Emma's half hug as she handed him five strips of jerky. "For the hike, Sven. Be careful. I hope you find your father."

"Thank you, Emma. Goodbye."

Sven turned to the door and peeked out. Lt. Castner was not in sight so he ran toward the trail that led from Sunrise City to Hope. He crouched in an alder thicket. He would need to be more careful because Lt. Castner knew he was in Sunrise City.

7

In his hiding place Sven pulled his collar up and his cap down as he endured the constant buzz of mosquitoes near his ears. He squished those that landed on his exposed face and hands.

He glanced upward toward the sun and prayed that he had not been late. If the lieutenant did not come before the sun circled beyond the tip of that tall spruce he would hike to Hope.

Sven recognized the straight posture and long stride as Lt. Castner walked from Sunrise City. The shorter, heavy man who had been at breakfast with the lieutenant jogged beside him. They slowed their pace as Sven watched.

"I'm sorry, Hicks," Sven heard Lt. Castner say as they neared the alder thicket. "That is how fast I usually walk. It's my military pace."

"If you walk that fast, Lieutenant, you will need a different guide. A guide is supposed to lead, not run to catch up." The man laughed at his own wit.

Sven smiled. Lt. Castner carried a heavy pack; the other man, Hicks, carried a small bundle, but he could not match the lieutenant's strides. Sven remembered how difficult that could be.

"All right, Hicks, you lead," Lt. Castner said as they passed Sven's hiding place.

Sven followed at a distance. Each time the two men stopped he hid off the trail and waited. The sun stood high in the sky when they arrived in Hope.

Sven cautiously shadowed Lt. Castner about the sprawling, busy mining town. Each time the lieutenant entered a building he watched outside.

He followed to where a small steamboat, the *Perry*, was docked near a stream that flowed into Turnagain Arm. Lt. Castner stood on deck talking to the ship's captain. After the lieutenant departed, Sven walked up the gangway.

"Hello, Boy," the captain greeted him. "What do you want?"

"I wondered where you are going. I am going to join my father in Circle City. I need a way across the inlet."

"You cannot get to Circle City from there, unless ..." the captain paused, "...unless you join that army officer that just left. He said he was going to make a trail to Circle City."

Sven smiled. "Where is he going?"

"I am taking him across Cook Inlet to Tyonek at high tide the day after tomorrow. Want to go along?"

"How much?"

"Two dollars. That includes a meal and a bunk for the night at Knik."

"Where's Knik?"

"On the Knik Arm of Cook Inlet. I intend to stop at the trading post there, and," the captain said and smiled, "to be the first captain to take his steamship into the Knik Arm. For two dollars you may share that adventure."

Sven felt into his almost empty coin purse and frowned. "How much if I don't eat and I sleep on deck?"

The captain looked at Sven. "How does one dollar sound? No, fifty cents with no bunk and no food. I'm going there anyway."

Sven smiled. "That sounds good. Thank you, Captain, thank you."

"Come aboard early, day after tomorrow. High tide is at eight-thirty."

"I'll be here, Captain."

Sven smiled as he left the *Perry*. For the next day and a half he did not need to shadow Lt. Castner.

What he needed was food. After being sure the lieutenant was not in the busy general store, he entered. With his remaining money, except for fifty cents, he bought hardtack and jerky, and, as an idea popped into his head, a box of matches.

Sven returned to the stream and walked uphill, looking for a place to fish. McGregor's string and hook were in his Mackinaw pocket. He found a deep, shaded pool at a bend in the stream, a pool similar to the one where he fished with McGregor. He snapped off a branch to use as a pole and tied his string to it. With a small piece of jerky as bait he jiggled his line into the water.

The line tightened and the tug on his pole happened quickly. As Sven tightened his grip he saw a silvery fish fighting for freedom. He yanked the pole up and back. The fish landed on the bank beside him.

Now what do I do? Sven wondered. He gathered leaves and grass, twigs and small branches to build a fire. Everything felt wet. He wasted four matches as he muttered to himself. "I need something dry, paper. Something like that curly bark. Maybe that will work."

He peeled bark from the tree and rebuilt his fire, bark for paper, twigs, larger branches, like he had watched the soldiers do at camp on Portage Bay. The bark ignited with the first match. Black smoke rolled up from the blaze and Sven fed larger branches into the fire.

With his small pocket knife he hacked the head from his fish and trimmed an alder branch into a point. He rammed the pointed branch lengthwise through the fish and held it over the fire.

"You, Boy, what are you doing on my claim?"

The angry voice startled Sven. He turned and looked into the face of a lean, tall, red-haired man holding a knife. "Your claim?"

"My claim. Do you know what happens to claim

jumpers? They get hanged. I could kill you myself for trying to find gold on my claim."

"I'm fishing," Sven said as he backed away. "Look in my duffel bag. I don't have any gold."

The man eyed Sven as he dumped out the contents of the duffel bag and poked through them.

"A man needs to protect his property," he said and tucked his knife into his boot top. "What are you doing here?"

Sven explained that he waited to depart on the *Perry* and decided to camp to save money. "My name is Sven Olafsen," he concluded.

The man, convinced that Sven was not a claim jumper, smiled. "Nice salmon, Sven, but it will take hours to cook that way. Let me show you."

Sven watched as the man placed a number of rocks in the fire, with a large flat one on the bottom. He pushed hot coals over them. Then he pulled the salmon off Sven's stick, sliced it down the middle and gutted it. He cut two pieces from the sides and placed them on the flat rock with other rocks and coals over them.

"They will bake fast there," he said. "Fish roasts fast, so don't leave them too long."

The remainder of the salmon he cut into strips. "Hang these above the fire. They will dry out and cook slowly and pick up a tasty smoky flavor."

As Sven draped the strips over his stick, the man cut two branches with crotches and pushed them into the ground. "Hang your stick across there."

Sven obeyed the directions. "I really thank you, Sir. I would never have thought of doing what you taught me."

The now friendly man smiled. "Don't call me sir. Call me Pat, short for Patrick, like all my friends do."

"I will, Sir, er, Pat. May I stay here until the *Perry* leaves?"

"You may stay, Sven, and I'll teach you how to pan for gold after we eat your salmon."

With his knife Pat raked the coals and rocks away from the salmon. "Got anything to eat with?"

"No," Sven answered.

"Peel off two pieces of bark." Pat pointed at the tree where Sven had found his fire starter. "Birch bark peels easily. We'll slide pieces under the salmon."

"It's hot," Pat warned as he handed one piece to Sven, "and delicious. Add more wood to your fire to smoke those strips."

Sven stoked the fire; the damp wood provided heat and smoke.

"Looks good," Pat said. "Now let me show you how to pan for gold."

Pat walked into a shallow spot in the stream, scooped up a small amount of gravel, and slowly swished water around in it. "Gold is heaviest and sinks to the bottom." He swished water through the gravel several times, with stops to throw out pebbles that did not swish out.

"Now look." He brought the pan to shore. A thin layer of silt remained in the pan. "See there, Sven, those bright specs are gold."

Pat took the specs out on the tip of a finger and added them to a small half full bottle. "Gold dust, Sven. I get some every day. Now you know why I don't want anyone on my claim. Ready to try?"

"Can I try it from here?" Sven did not want to get his shoes wet.

"Sure."

Sven scooped up a small amount of gravel from the stream bottom. Under Pat's supervision he swished water through the gravel. When he finished there were no shining specs, no gold.

"Try again."

Pat watched while Sven panned.

"Stop!" Pat grabbed Sven's arm as he held a pebble ready to flip back into the stream. Pat snatched it from his hand.

8

"THAT'S a nugget! Gold!" Pat held the nugget in front of Sven's eyes before tucking it into a pouch beneath his shirt. "Keep at it, Sven. You're lucky, I know you are."

"Maybe so." Sven laughed and scooped up more gravel. He panned until Pat prepared to return to town.

"You did say I could stay here tonight, didn't you, Pat?" Sven asked,

"Sure," Pat said, "and I will leave my pan here. Maybe you will find another nugget for me."

"I doubt it. Thanks, Pat."

Sven ate hardtack and jerky and a strip of smoked salmon. Delicious.

He caught a second salmon, hacked it into strips with his knife and hung them over the fire. He sniffed smoked salmon as he curled up under his slicker.

In the morning Sven caught and roasted a small fish in the coals. After eating he panned for gold. He saved the gold flecks on a piece of birch bark. He placed two pebble sized nuggets with the flecks.

"Having any luck?" Pat asked as he walked up behind Sven.

"A little." Sven swished the water from the pan and plucked up two flecks. "Here." He placed the flecks on the bark and handed it to Pat.

"Two nuggets! I knew you were lucky! I knew it when you found that nugget yesterday. I knew it."

"Why am I lucky?" Sven asked.

"Why? I have been here a year and only found five nuggets. You found three in two days."

Sven stared at nuggets. "I thought you found them every day."

Pat laughed. "Most men never find enough to get rich, or even enough to return home. I am so sure that you are lucky that I bought these with the nugget you found. I want you to be my partner."

Sven opened the bag Pat handed him. He pulled out a miner's pan, a sheathed knife, and a fork.

"That is all you need," Pat said. "You can share my cabin."

"I can't do that. I am going to find my father."

"Think about it," Pat said. "Think about it as we pan."

Pat stood in midstream. Sven panned from the shore. When he found another nugget an idea popped into his head.

"Pat, you should pan near shore."

"Why?"

"The swift current carries pebbles and gold with it. They settle in the slower water. Try it."

"Maybe you're right. I'll try it," Pat said.

Many pans later Pat grasped a tooth-size nugget. "You are lucky, Sven! And smart! You have to be my partner."

"I wish I could, Pat, but I plan to find my father. I'm leaving in the morning."

Pat nodded. "I thought you would say that. Keep these nuggets you found." He handed the three nuggets to Sven. "They are worth at least thirty dollars each. Don't let anyone cheat you."

"But they're yours," Sven argued.

"I'll find more because of you. Even after you leave you will be lucky for me. I'll thank you every time I find a nugget."

After Pat left him, Sven fingered the three nuggets before placing them in his empty purse. With the long drawstring he tied it around his neck and tucked it back beneath his shirt. He ate smoked salmon and hardtack before curling up under his slicker. Should I offer to pay Lt. Castner to take me to Circle City, he wondered before he fell asleep.

———

At first light Sven hurried to the *Perry* and walked aboard. Behind the wheelhouse he found a place to sit out of sight of the dock. He hoped Lt. Castner would not see him until they departed for Tyonek.

"Here so soon?" The captain leaned from a wheel-house window.

"You said to be early."

"That I did. Welcome aboard. We leave as soon as Lt. Castner arrives."

"Do you have bunks left?" Sven asked.

"Plenty. Do you have money now?"

"I have ..."

"Captain?" Lt. Castner's shout interrupted Sven, and the captain disappeared from the window.

"Come aboard. We're ready to leave. Steam's up and the tide is high."

Sven smiled and stayed sitting. After the *Perry* steamed out into Turnagain Arm, he walked around the deck.

"Good morning, Lieutenant Castner, Mr. Hicks," he greeted the two men as they stood at the stern rail.

Lt. Castner whirled around and stared. "Sven? What? How? The waitress in Sunrise City asked me about you. 'Sven Olafsen,' she said. Had your name wrong."

Sven suppressed a laugh. "Are you surprised, Sir? I want to go to Circle City with you, and my name is Sven Olafsen."

"Not Johanson?"

"I lied to you. I ran away from home because I want to

57

find my father. Our last letter from him was dated in August." Sven bit his lip and fought back tears as he told how he had left his mother at the train depot in Seattle. "I have to go with you to Circle City."

Before Lt. Castner could answer, Mr. Hicks asked, "Do you know what you are getting into? How do you know me?"

"I heard Lieutenant Castner say your name when I followed you from Sunrise, Mr. Hicks," Sven answered. "I don't know what I am getting into, but I intend to find my father."

Hicks shook his head. "You are very brave or very stupid, maybe both."

Lt. Castner, agitated, clenched his fists. "He is determined. Twice I arranged for him to return to Seattle. Maybe it's not too late to try again, once we arrive in Tyonek. Think about this, Sven. Does you mother need you more than you need to find your father? You were smart enough to get this far; you could find your way from Seattle to Minnesota."

"You don't understand." Sven fought his tears and anger as he returned to his seat beside the wheelhouse.

The captain stuck his head from the window. "What were you asking about a bunk? Do you have money now?"

"Gold."

The captain smiled. "Gold? Come in here."

Sven reached beneath his shirt and felt in his drawstring purse. He pulled out the smallest gold nugget.

"I found this," he said as he entered the wheelhouse.

"Where?"

"In the gravel by the river."

"Where?"

"A short way from your ship."

"Hmm." The captain took the nugget and bit it. "You may have a bunk and meals for it."

"And how much more?" Sven asked. "I need money."

The captain smiled and said, "Can't fool you, can I? Ten dollars."

"Not enough." Pat had said not to accept less than thirty dollars. "Fifty with the bunk and meals."

"Twenty-five."

"Thirty-five."

"Thirty-five," the captain agreed. "You drive a hard bargain." He pulled a money belt from around his waist, tucked in the nugget, and handed Sven the money.

Sven smiled and wondered if he had made a good bargain. He tucked the money into his pouch and watched the shoreline.

———

"We stay here overnight," the captain told his passengers as they tied up against the bank at Knik. "We leave with high tide tomorrow. I have business." He walked down the gangplank and toward the trading post.

"I'm going ashore," Mr. Hicks said. "I'll spend the night with my wife."

"Your wife?" Lt. Castner asked in surprise.

"I married a native girl last summer," Mr. Hicks said. "but I haven't seen her since February."

"I'm staying on board," Lt. Castner said. "I need to write my reports and work on my maps."

Sven followed Mr. Hicks down the gangplank. He stared at the native Tanaina as he walked, and they stared at him. He wished he knew what they said. To avoid their stares he entered the trading post.

He listened to the Perry's captain and the trading post's owner bargain.

"All three stacks of furs, Mr. McDermott," he heard the captain say.

"You win. I will have my helpers load the furs and bring back my supplies. You drive a hard bargain."

Sven smiled. That is what the captain had said to him. Maybe he could drive a hard bargain here too.

"Mr. McDermott, how much are these boots?" he asked.

"Twenty-five dollars. They are the best: waterproof,

seal skin outside, caribou fur inside, soft and warm. Try them on." Mr. McDermott was a good salesman.

Sven found a pair that fit. "I'll trade my shoes for these." His best boots were on the *Perry*.

"Your shoes and twenty dollars."

"Fifteen," Sven said, "and include two pair of stockings and a pair of gloves."

"Those gloves are beaver, waterproof, with warm fur inside. Boots, stockings, and gloves for your shoes and twenty dollars."

"Too much. Fifteen," Sven said.

"Where are you going?" Mr. McDermott asked.

"Circle City."

"It gets mighty cold there. Twenty dollars, and a bargain. You'll need the warm boots and gloves."

"You drive a hard bargain." Sven paid the twenty dollars.

As he returned to the Perry, he wondered if he could convince Lt. Castner to enlist him into the army.

9

"LIEUTENANT Castner, Sir, I want to join the army," Sven said as he and the lieutenant leaned on the ship rail.

"Join the army?" The lieutenant snapped erect and faced Sven.

"Yes, Sir. So I can go with you to Circle City."

"How old are you?"

"Eighteen."

Sven felt his face redden as Lt. Castner stared into his eyes. His blushing, as always, told that he lied.

"Sven, be honest. How old are you?"

"Fifteen in September."

"Only fourteen. Are you sure you want to join the army? If you join, you won't be allowed to return home with your father. You will need to stay in the army," Lt. Castner said. "I thought you would want to go home to your mother."

"You mean I couldn't leave when I find my father?"

"You would be a deserter. If you were caught you might be shot."

Sven bit his lip as he stared into the serious face of the tall lieutenant. "Shot?"

"Yes, Sven, and you may never find your father. Alaska is a large territory. Circle City is still far away." He draped his arm over Sven's shoulder. "Your mother needs a man in the house. With your father gone, you must be that man. I will help you find a way home."

A man? Nobody has ever called me a man before, Sven thought. I will be a man, but a man who will find his father.

"My mother needs my father." Sven shook the lieutenant's arm from his shoulders. "I will find him."

Sven walked to the prow and watched the passing shore as the *Perry* steamed from Knik toward Tyonek. Far to the west and north towered snowcapped mountains. Nearer, the land they approached appeared flat and barren except for a few cabins and a cluster of gray canvas tents.

"Tyonek," the captain said as they approached. "Drop anchor."

His crewmen lowered a boat and rowed Sven, Lt. Castner, and Mr. Hicks to shore.

"Come along, Sven," Lt. Castner said. "We'll find a place to camp until you go back to Seattle."

"I am not going back."

"Then you are on your own. Come along, Hicks. We need to find a place large enough for my army company. Captain Glenn should soon be here with our men and supplies."

Sven walked toward the cabins.

"Are you going to the Yukon?" he asked each man he met. "I have to join my father in Circle City."

"You cannot get to Circle City from here," each man answered and laughed. "Go home, Boy."

It can be done, Sven thought. Lieutenant Castner is going to do it, and so am I.

He returned to the beach where winter storms had piled driftwood. He lit a fire behind the gnarled root section of a large tree trunk. He leaned back against the tree, ate hardtack, jerky, and smoked salmon, and wondered if he should return home.

He shook his head to get rid of the thought. Some way, some how, he would follow the army to Circle City. As he planned he thought of his friend Mac. He fell asleep imagining how Private McGregor might help him.

———

The early rising sun of the lengthening arctic days awakened Sven. As he ate he listened to squawking gulls as they skimmed above the water or fought for food on the beach. He watched white beluga whales swim in the deeper water. Far to the north one snow-covered mountain towered above the other peaks. On the beach nearby he saw a second cluster of tents.

Sven hiked to the tents. Perhaps miners camped there were going to the Yukon.

"Any one going to Circle City?" he asked some miners.

"You can't get there from here, not up the Susitna River. You can't get over the mountains," one man said.

Sven saw two miners hiking toward a river. "Is that the Susitna River?" he asked.

"That's it."

"Where you going, Boy?" one miner asked as Sven walked toward the river. "You can't get to Circle City."

"I'm going fishing."

Sven donned his new sealskin boots to hike through the marshland before the river. Upstream he found a tree leaning over the water and climbed out on it. With jerky for bait he caught three salmon.

He squatted at the river's edge and panned for gold. With not a single fleck of gold in five tries, he quit and hiked back to the rocky beach. He started a fire to heat rocks before cutting up his fish, one into chucks to roast in the hot coals, and two into strips for smoking.

"Sven?"

Surprised, Sven pivoted away from his fire. Lt. Castner and Mr. Hicks walked toward him on the beach.

"What are you doing here at Ladd's Station?" the lieutenant asked.

"Trying to find someone traveling to Circle City."

"Did you find anyone?" Mr. Hicks asked. "You can't get there from here. You have to follow the Matanuska River. The mountains are too high north of here. They are not as high north of the Matanuska. Where did you catch your salmon?"

"In the river." Sven pointed toward the mouth of the Susitna. "Why are you here, Sir?"

"We needed a better place to camp," Lt. Castner answered. "We will need fresh water and grass for the mules and horses, and firewood. They're all here and not in Tyonek."

"Nice work on your fire, Sven," Mr. Hicks said. "Where did you learn to smoke salmon? Did you ever taste smoked salmon, Lieutenant? It's good. Tastes better with green wood smoke but this will do. Can I try some?"

He broke off a piece before Sven could answer.

"Not quite ready yet." He smiled at Sven. "We could use a good fisherman and cook, Lieutenant."

"I have some salmon roasting in the fire," Sven said. If the lieutenant would listen to Mr. Hicks he might get to Circle City. "It should be ready. Care to try some."

"I will," Mr. Hicks said and sat down on a driftwood log.

Sven scraped back the glowing coals and rocks and knifed the chunks of salmon into his pan. Mr. Hicks and Lt. Castner brushed off the ashes and tasted the fresh roasted fish.

"Delicious," Mr. Hicks declared. "What do you think, Lieutenant? Do we hire a cook?"

"Where did you learn to cook like this?" Lt. Castner asked.

"I am not much of a cook," Sven said. "Pat, a miner in Hope, taught me this, and this is all I know."

"He can learn more," Mr. Hicks said.

"I will think about it," Lt. Castner said. "Sven, you may camp with us until Captain Glenn arrives."

"Thank you, Sir," Sven said. He smiled at Mr. Hicks who winked at him.

———

For three days Sven fished, and roasted and smoked

salmon. At midday of their fourth day at Ladd's Station, Sven saw the *Valencia* steaming toward Tyonek. He did not want to see Captain Adams, not after he had agreed to be fireman and then jumped ship.

"It's the *Valencia*, Sven." Lt. Castner placed his hand on Sven's shoulder. "Your ship back to Seattle."

"You're not going to hire me as cook?"

"No, you should go back to your mother."

"May I go with you if I pay you?" Sven asked. "I have some gold."

"No, not even if you pay me."

"Get your things. We will hurry to Tyonek and meet the *Valencia*." Lt. Castner pushed Sven in the direction of the tent. "Hicks?"

Sven ran to the tent as Lt. Castner walked to where Mr. Hicks sat on a log and whittled.

Sven grabbed his duffel bag from the tent and sneaked into the trees. He zigzagged from tree to tree, keeping out of sight. He lay in deep grass behind a log and watched the beach. He heard Lt. Castner call but did not answer.

He watched the lieutenant walk toward Tyonek. After the lieutenant left the beach he crawled from his hiding place and joined Mr. Hicks.

"You are determined, aren't you?" Mr. Hicks grinned and winked at him. "I like your spunk, Sven. I hope you join us."

The two sat together and watched a small boat with two men row to the *Valencia*. "Must be the lieutenant," Mr. Hicks said.

They watched one man row back to shore and the *Valencia* steam away in the direction it had come. "Now what?" Mr. Hicks said. "I do believe the lieutenant has left us. Let's eat some of your salmon."

Sven smiled. It seemed as if all Mr. Hicks liked to do was eat and talk, and he preferred eating. Sven enjoyed listening to Mr. Hick's stories of his adventures in Alaska and his previous trip up the Matanuska River. "That's the way we have to go to reach Circle City, Sven," he said.

Sven nodded; if the lieutenant did not return he would ask Mr. Hicks to be his guide.

———

As they sat and ate at noon the next day, a different ship steamed into view.

"Maybe we haven't been left," Mr. Hicks said as the *Walcott* passed Tyonek and turned toward Ladd's Station. Soldiers stood at the ship's rail. "Looks like we are having company."

"And I am going to hide, so Lieutenant Castner cannot ship me back to Seattle." Sven ran into the woods.

10

Sven watched two small boats shuttling to shore from the *Walcott*. It took many trips to land the soldiers with their supplies.

Sven retreated deeper into hiding as Lt. Castner led soldiers with saws and axes toward him. They sawed down spruce trees and chopped off branches. In the twilight a bugle command called them to camp.

Sven hid when soldiers dragged the logs to the beach the next morning. As miners watched from the bluff, he sneaked in among them. The soldiers built a raft and towed it to the *Walcott*. A side hatch opened and Sven recognized the mule handler, Dillon. He led a horse down a narrow gangplank and onto the raft.

A soldier held the horse's halter as Dillon reentered the ship. He returned leading a mule. The mule balked with its first step onto the gangplank. Dillon pulled on its lead rope and soldiers, avoiding kicks, pushed from behind. The mule would not move.

Using his gruff voice, Sven shouted, "Dillon, you forgot to blindfold the mule."

Dillon pulled a kerchief from his pocket and wrapped

it over the mule's eyes. The blindfolded animal followed him onto the raft. In five trips Dillon ferried the animals to shore.

Sven watched from the bank as the *Walcott* steamed away.

———

"You, Boy. Where's the man who shouted about blindfolding the mules?"

Sven stood up and replied in his gruff voice, "Dillon, I shouted at you.".

"You?" Dillon asked. "You sound like the man who helped load the mules in Haines. You look like the fireman who jumped ship in Portage Bay."

Sven laughed. "That's me, mule handler, stowaway, fireman, runaway."

"Captain Glenn wants to see you. I think he will offer you a job. Are you willing to leave your miner friends?"

"They are not my friends. I am joining my father in Circle City and the only way for me to get there is with the soldiers. I followed Lieutenant Castner here."

"Come along," Dillon said.

Several soldiers greeted Sven as he walked through camp.

"Hello, Sven. Good to see you." McGregor walked over and patted Sven on the back. "I hoped I would see you again."

"It's good to see you, Mac."

"So, are you going with us?"

"I don't know. Dillon thinks I am."

"Sure he is," Mr. Hicks said and winked at Sven, "Sven is going to be camp fisherman and cook."

"No, he's not," Dillon said. "He's going to help with the mules."

"It looks like you will stay," McGregor said and grinned.

Mr. Hicks, McGregor, and other soldiers followed Dillon and Sven to Capt. Glenn's tent. The captain, with lieutenants Castner and Learnard, watched them approach.

Sven stared at the stocky uniformed captain. The

captain's eyes twinkled and a smile played around the corner of his lips.

"This is the man who shouted for me to blindfold the mules, Captain Glenn," Dillon said. "He's the one you said I should try to hire."

Sven smiled at the captain.

"He's only a boy," Capt. Glenn said. He looked closely at Sven. "Lieutenant Castner, isn't this the boy you tried to send home from Haines?"

"Yes, he is, Sir. His name is Sven Olafsen."

"And isn't he the boy who disappeared from the *Valencia* in Portage Bay?"

"Yes, Sir."

"Have you helped him, Lieutenant? Alaska is a hard place for a boy by himself."

"I did not help him, Sir."

"Then why is he here?"

"I am going to find my father, Captain," Sven said before Lt. Castner could answer. "He is in Circle City and you are going to Circle City, so I want to go with you. I will help with the mules and do other work if you let me come."

"Captain, Sir, he is good at handling mules," Dillon said.

"He can fish and cook, Captain," Mr. Hicks said and winked at Sven. "You should taste his smoked salmon. Give him a piece, Sven."

"It sounds as if you have friends, Sven," Capt. Glenn said. "If you are what they say, we can use you."

"Try some, Sir." Sven handed strips of smoked salmon to the captain and two lieutenants.

Lt. Castner immediately bit off a piece.

"Is it good, Lieutenant?" Capt. Glenn asked. "Did you have some before?"

"Yes, Sir. It is good."

"Do you want the boy to go with you, Lieutenant?" the captain's eyes sparkled and he grinned at Lt. Castner. "He wants to go to Circle City and you haven't had success in sending him home. Seems as if he outwitted you more than once."

"He is determined, Sir."

"And his smoked salmon is delicious." The captain smiled at Sven and squeezed his shoulder. "Think it over, Lieutenant. It is your decision. If he comes, he goes with you. Sven, do you have more salmon?"

"He can catch more, Captain," Mr. Hicks said. "He can serve you roast salmon tonight. Go catch some fresh salmon, Sven." He winked and whispered, "If Captain Glenn likes you, Lieutenant Castner will have to take you along."

Sven smiled. "Salmon for dinner, Sir. Excuse me." He picked up his duffel bag and trotted toward the river.

———

From his tree perch Sven saw salmon swimming near midstream. None swam beneath him.

If getting to Circle City depends on catching fish, Sven thought, I have to be where the fish are. He climbed down and tightened the laces on his sealskin boots. He felt the coldness of the water as he waded toward midstream.

He jiggled his jerky-baited hook near a salmon. The salmon snatched it and tried to swim away. He yanked it from the water.

"Great catch."

Sven looked to where McGregor watched from shore. He waded toward him. "Thanks. Mac. If you came to fish, they're out here."

"I'll wait here. Isn't the water cold?"

"I have these waterproof, fur-lined boots, from the trading post in Knik," Sven said. "I barely feel the cold."

He handed his fish to McGregor and waded out to catch another.

As Sven delivered his eleventh fish to shore, McGregor said, "Time to go. You have another visitor." He pointed across the river.

Sven gaped at the large brown bear. "How long has it been there?"

"I don't know; I spotted it a minute ago. Anyway, eleven fish will feed everyone. Let's go."

Sven stared at the bear. "Thanks for coming, Mac. I never thought about watching for bears."

McGregor grinned at him. "So, sometimes I'm in the right place at the right time. As for you, you need to be alert. If a bear wants your fish, let him have it. Now, let's get these fish to camp."

Sven showed McGregor and Private Blitch how to cut the salmon into chunks. At each campfire he showed the soldiers how to bury the pieces in rocks to roast in the coals. He buried the largest pieces in the fire by Capt. Glenn's tent and tended them.

"Your roast salmon was delicious, Sven," Capt. Glenn said after the meal. "Do you still want to get to Circle City?"

"More than anything, Sir. May I go with you?"

"After you left this morning, Private McGregor talked to me. He said he would be responsible for you."

"He's a good friend, Sir. He taught me how to fish."

Capt. Glenn smiled. "I talked to Lieutenant Castner, twisted his arm a little, and he agreed to take you with him."

"Thank you, Sir."

"Will you obey him?"

"Yes, Sir."

"Good. I know he tried to have you return to your mother, Sven. That is because he likes you. He wanted you to do what was best, which would be to go home. Do you understand that?"

"Yes, Sir."

"It will be difficult to cut a trail to Circle City and we may turn back. It will be dangerous and you might be killed. Do you still want to go?"

"Yes, Sir."

"Lieutenant Castner says you are determined." Capt. Glenn grasped Sven's shoulders and looked into his eyes. "You are now under his command. You will help with the mules and do whatever he orders you to do. Report to him now."

"Oh, thank you, Captain. I will."

Sven bounded away and burst into Lt. Castner's tent. "Captain Glenn said I am going with you. Thank you, Sir. He said you would give me orders."

Lt. Castner looked up from a map and scowled. "Your first order is to stand straight and be quiet. Your second order is that from now on you ask if you may enter my tent."

"Yes, Sir. I'm sorry."

"You will share a tent with Private McGregor and three more soldiers. You may go."

"May I ask a question, Sir?"

"What is it?"

"When do we start for Circle City?"

"In a few days. We need to prepare first. Now please leave."

"Yes, Sir."

Sven dashed from the tent. "Mac," he yelled, "where are you? I'm going to Circle City with you!"

Part Two

DETERMINATION

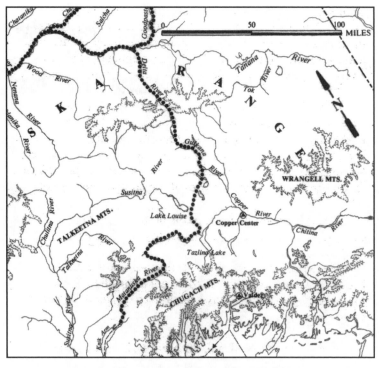

Overland, northeast from the Knik Arm
of Cook Inlet, up the Matanuska River valley,
northward past Lake Louise, over the Alaska Range,
and down the Delta River to the Nenana River,
June, July, and August, 1898.

II

A blaring bugle awakened Sven. He dressed quickly and lined up with McGregor and the other soldiers.

"'Tention," one soldier ordered as Capt. Glenn approached from his tent.

"Men," Capt. Glenn said, "today we begin our final preparations for developing trails to the Yukon River. Lieutenants Castner and Learnard will divide you into two units. Lieutenant Learnard's squad will travel by boat up the Susitna River as far as possible and then proceed overland.

"Lieutenant Castner will lead his squad up the Matanuska River valley and then north across the mountains. He will have one extra man with him. Most of you have met Sven Olafsen. I have given him permission to accompany Lieutenant Castner to Circle City where he will join his father. Private McGregor has volunteered to be responsible for his welfare."

Sven looked at McGregor and smiled. McGregor, face forward, stood ramrod stiff. Sven copied his posture.

Capt. Glenn spoke quietly with the two lieutenants, saluted, and returned to his tent.

"At ease," Lt. Castner ordered.

Sven copied the wide-legged stance as the soldiers relaxed and listened.

"These men will form my squad: Corporal Young, Privates McGregor, Ayres, Woodruff, Evans, Powers, Dillinger, and VanSchoonhoven, and Sven Olafsen. Fall out and assemble before my tent."

Sven walked with McGregor and lined up with the men before Lt. Castner's tent.

"'Tention," Corporal Young ordered.

Sven stood rigidly with the soldiers.

"At ease," Lt. Castner said. "You will have one hour for breakfast. After that we will divide supplies with Lieutenant Learnard's men and stack ours on the beach. When the Perry arrives we will board and transfer our supplies to a base camp on the Knik Arm of the inlet. You all know Dillon; he will be in charge of our animals. McGregor and Sven will be his assistants. Some of you have met Hicks; he will be our guide as we cut our trail up the Matanuska valley. He is the only non-native to have journeyed to the glacier where the river begins. 'Tention. Fall out.

"McGregor, Sven."

"Yes, Sir," McGregor answered and stopped.

"Yes, Sir." Sven copied McGregor.

"I have a special assignment for you today," Lt. Castner said. "There won't be much work with the animals. See how many salmon you can catch. That smoked salmon tastes good and I like a treat before I retire each evening."

"Yes, Sir," McGregor said.

"Yes, Sir," Sven echoed.

———

After breakfast McGregor, carrying a saw, led Sven into the woods. "We'll stay out of sight, Sven, so the other men won't know we've gone fishing. They won't be jealous if they think we are cutting fire wood. When we serve fish tonight, they won't complain that we didn't help move supplies."

"We better catch a lot of them," Sven said. "You fish and I'll cut them up."

With birch bark and driftwood, Sven lit a fire on the river bank. With four forked sticks and two poles he prepared to smoke strips of salmon. He sawed down a small tree and fed the green wood into the fire to provide more smoke. Through the day, he sliced fish and stoked the fire.

"Save the rest of the fish," McGregor said when the smoking racks were full. "We need some to roast."

The *Perry* lay anchored off shore when Sven and McGregor returned to camp late in the afternoon.

After the evening meal, Lt. Castner called his platoon together and said, "We will load at high tide tomorrow. Get a good night's sleep and be ready to work in the morning. Dismissed."

———

As the tide rose the next morning, the *Perry* steamed closer to shore. With the raft anchored to the beach and the gangplank extended, the men carried supplies onto the deck.

"Dillon, Sven," Lt. Castner ordered, "fetch the horse and mules."

"Yes, Sir," Sven replied. He followed Dillon to the grassy meadow where the animals were hobbled.

"The lieutenant says we get the roan horse, and four mules," Dillon said, and pointed. "Sven, get those two mules."

"Come on, mules, we're going for a boat ride." Sven talked quietly as he tied ropes to the mules' halters. "Hold still. That's a good mule." He unhobbled their forelegs and led them toward the ship.

"Hurry with those animals," the captain of the Perry called. "The tide is going out."

Sven stopped on the beach. "Hold this." He handed one lead rope to Pvt. Ayres.

He draped his kerchief over the eyes of the other mule. "Come on, mule." He tugged as the mule balked on the unsteady raft. "Come on, there is nothing to fear."

He led the mule onto the deck and tied it to a railing on the wheelhouse wall with its head away from the water.

"Don't tie it there," the captain said.

"I have to, Sir," Sven replied, "so it doesn't see the water and get spooked." The mule stood quietly as he removed the blindfold and hurried after his second mule.

"Sven, stay on board and look after the animals," Lt. Castner ordered when the horse and mules were on deck. "The rest of us will board later."

The *Perry's* crew pulled up the gangway and the ship steamed toward deeper water to wait out the low tide. Sven fed the horse and four mules and shoveled manure over the side of the ship as they waited for the next high tide.

———

"I brought you something," McGregor said when he boarded the ship in the unending twilight of the early June night. He handed Sven an army backpack. "Can't have your carrying your duffel bag all the way to Circle City. You will need your hands free for leading animals and other work."

"Where is my duffel bag?" Sven asked. "I left it in the tent."

"It's in your pack."

Sven sighed with relief. All that he owned, extra shirt and trousers, new boots and gloves, his Mackinaw and slicker, was in the duffel bag. Using his pack for a pillow, he lay on deck with the soldiers as the *Perry* steamed northeast toward Knik.

———

At mid-morning, as the tide rose, Sven stood at the ship's rail looking for Knik, the native village. Before they reached the village he heard Lt. Castner say, "There, Captain. Can you land us there?" The lieutenant pointed toward a low spot on the shoreline.

"I'll try," the captain of the *Perry* replied.

As the tide rose, the captain inched the ship against the bank. "Get your men off fast, Lieutenant," he said as his crew lowered the gangplank to the bank. "I don't want to be stranded here."

"Hurry, men," Lt. Castner said. "We don't have much time."

Sven, Dillon, and McGregor led the mules and horse down the gangplank, tied them to a long lead rope, and hobbled them. The other men began carrying packs and supplies from the ship.

"Lieutenant Castner, Sir," Sven called when he saw the men passing each other on the narrow gangplank, "have the men use a relay line. It will go faster if they pass supplies from man to man."

Lt. Castner stared at Sven for a second and nodded. "Men, form a line and pass the supplies to shore."

Sven stayed with McGregor and stacked supplies at the end of the line.

"We will establish our supply camp here, Men," Lt. Castner said as the *Perry* steamed away. "Clear a large enough area."

Through the afternoon and early evening, Sven worked with the soldiers as they hacked away brush and small trees and pulled out roots. They leveled hummocks of dirt and set up tents for themselves and their supplies.

"Great work, Men," Lt. Castner praised them as they ate their late evening meal. "Get a good night's sleep. We begin cutting trail tomorrow."

———

In the morning Sven helped Dillon currycomb the horse and mules. The animals, after a month of rest and a week of fresh grass for food, looked healthier than when Sven helped load them into the *Valencia* in Haines. He talked to each mule as he combed it, and they cocked their ears to listen.

Mosquitoes swarmed around Sven's head as he worked.

He swatted at them and brushed them from the heads and backs of the animals. He watched the soldiers as they prepared packs for themselves and the animals. They swatted at mosquitoes and swore.

"Load up, Men," Lt. Castner ordered after they ate their lunch. "Let's get away from these bloodsucking mosquitoes."

The soldiers began chopping and sawing through alder and willow thickets. As they worked they continued to swear and swat mosquitoes. They slogged through soft turf that moved beneath their feet and turned to mud that pulled at their boots.

In the lower spots the mules, carrying heavy packs, sank into the mud.

"Dratted mud, stupid mule." Dillon tugged at the lead rope of one mule. "Move."

"Come on, Jack. You can do it. Pull," Sven whispered into his mule's ear. "You can do it."

But Jack and the other mules sank deeper into the mud.

"Unload them," Lt. Castner ordered.

12

SVEN unloaded Jack and two soldiers carried the mule's heavy packs to firm ground. More soldiers helped with the other mules and the horse.

"Come on, Jack." Step by step Sven jerked his own feet from the mud as he tugged on Jack's lead rope. On firm ground he reloaded Jack and helped reload the other mules.

"Drats. Not again." Dillon swore when the mules bogged down a second time. "Stupid mules. Stupid mosquitoes. Lieutenant Castner, we need help here."

The soldiers swore at the mules and swatted mosquitoes as they unloaded and reloaded the mules. Cutting trail was difficult without battling mud, mules, and mosquitoes. The soldiers complained and suggested to Lt. Castner that they turn back.

"We're all going to die from loss of blood," said one.

"Yeah," agreed another, "these mosquitoes will eat us alive."

"Not before we all disappear in a mud hole. No one will ever know what happened to us."

Sven wondered if Lt. Castner would turn back. He watched the lieutenant walk ahead and use his hatchet to slice strips of bark from trees. He cut white blaze marks every thirty to fifty feet for the trail makers to follow. After blazing several trees, he would stride back, write in a small book, and work with the men.

"Complaining doesn't make work easier," Lt. Castner said. "We have a long way to go. What kind of soldiers are you?"

Sven smiled. "Come on, mules. We have a long way to go. The lieutenant wants to get to Circle City as much as I do." He stroked the mules' noses, cracked dry mud from their legs and brushed mosquitoes from their backs.

He followed with the mules as Lt. Castner led his trail makers into the village of Knik.

"Wait here," Lt. Castner ordered as he entered the trading post.

Native Tanaina clustered around the soldiers and stared at the mules.

"Why lead funny moose?" one man asked Sven.

"Mules," Sven answered. "They are mules, not moose."

"Where you go?" an old man asked.

"To the Yukon River," Cpl. Young answered. "We are making a trail."

The old man shook his head. "Not go. Poison insects. High mountains. Freeze. Bigfoot eat." He held his hands wide apart to show the size of Bigfoot's feet.

The soldiers listened and laughed.

"White man crazy," the old man said. The other natives nodded in agreement and walked away.

A teenage native ran toward the waiting soldiers.

"Mr. Hicks!" he called as Lt. Castner stepped from the trading post door. "Where you go?"

"I'm their guide, Billy," Mr. Hicks answered. "We are making a trail up the Matanuska River."

Sven looked at the black haired, dark-eyed boy dressed in animal skin pants and a shirt from the trading post.

"Billy go?" Billy asked.

"Who is he?" Lt. Castner asked Mr. Hicks.

"Billy is my brother-in-law, my wife's brother."

"Tell him we don't need another boy along," Castner said. "One is enough."

"Billy work," Billy said.

"He could be useful," Mr. Hicks said. "We can use an

interpreter. Billy understands English and knows the native language."

Agitated, Lt. Castner clenched and unclenched his fists until he nodded and said, "I guess it won't hurt. How soon can you be ready to leave, Billy?"

"Ready now. Billy get things."

Sven smiled. It might be fun to have a boy about his own age on the trip.

"Men, I bought something for you," Lt. Castner said as Billy ran off. "Sven, pass these around."

"Mosquito netting," Lt. Castner said as Sven passed one to each man. "It should keep the mosquitoes off your face and necks. If you wear your gloves you will be protected."

Sven pulled his mosquito netting down over his cap. He laughed as he looked at the men; they made a weird looking company.

"No more complaining," Lt. Castner said. "Billy can catch up, so let's go."

He led the way from the village as the native men laughed and called after them.

Sven led two mules and listened to the calls.

"Watch out for Bigfoot."

"Funny moose, Boy. Bigfoot eat moose. You see."

"Bigfoot get you, Billy," one man called as Billy ran to join the soldiers. "You no come back."

The soldiers laughed and waved and called "Goodbye."

Sven did not laugh. He wondered if there were such an animal as Bigfoot. He had heard of similar beasts that lived in the mountains of Washington and Oregon.

Through the day he led the mules forward, following the trail cutters. Lt. Castner, Mr. Hicks, and Billy walked ahead, blazing trees, marking the way for the soldiers to cut the trail. The soldiers chopped brush and sawed down trees as they followed.

They swore less and swatted fewer mosquitoes.

Sven swatted less but sweat dampened his cap and shirt. Bundled up as he was, his body heat could not escape. However, he felt less sorry for himself than for the mules. The mosquitoes swarmed around their eyes and ears and bite them continuously. Sven brushed and swatted, but it seemed that for each mosquito he killed two others took its place.

Mud plagued Sven, Dillon, and the mules. At each mud hole the mules had to be unloaded and their packs carried to firm ground, and the mules pulled from the mud and reloaded. McGregor, Ayres, and VanSchoonhoven helped with the animals.

Sven did not join the soldiers in complaining about the miserable mud and mosquitoes. He had asked to be there. But he sighed with relief when Lt. Castner called a halt as the sun descended in the northwestern sky.

"It's nine-thirty. We will camp here tonight, Men," the lieutenant said as they gathered on the bank of a small stream.

"You have done well and we have made a good start. We cut nine miles of trail today. Sven, start a fire. We will eat and then retire."

Sven, with Billy's help, collected wood and lit a fire. Privates Ayres and Woodruff served as cooks and the men ate greedily.

"I'm getting extra meat, here," Mr. Hicks said. He looked at Sven and Billy and winked as he held up his fork. Several mosquitoes clustered on the piece of potato which he popped into his mouth. "That's one way to kill the pests."

"Ugh," several of the soldiers responded, but other laughed.

There was no way to avoid the mosquitoes. The bloodsuckers swarmed around the food, and around the faces of the men who could not wear mosquito netting while they ate.

"I have a treat for you," Lt. Castner said as they finished eating. He passed a strip of smoked salmon to each man. "I don't know how long this will last. Thank Sven for it, and hope we find a stream or two where he can fish. Now get a good's night's rest. We have long days ahead of us."

Sven shared a tent with McGregor, Woodruff, Ayers, and VanSchoonhoven, and hundreds of mosquitoes.

"Who let in all the mosquitoes?" VanSchoonhoven complained. "It is bad enough to have to eat them."

The five killed as many of the mosquitoes as they could before trying to sleep. But buzzing and the frequent sound of slapping lasted through the night.

Without much sleep, Sven crawled from the tent early the next morning. He tended the mules and horse and led then to the stream to drink before he ate his own breakfast. He rubbed mud over them to relieve the irritation they might have from their mosquito bites and wondered if mosquitoes could bite through the mud.

Sweating, swearing at mules and mosquitoes, and grumbling, the soldiers toiled ten to twelve hours each day. They chopped and sawed through virgin forest of spruce and birch, alder, and willow. They trimmed felled trees and lay the logs side by side, forming corduroy trails through mud and swamp. They cut the trail up and over ridges as high as eight hundred feet. Lt. Castner paced off and marked the distance in miles.

"Good work today, Men," the lieutenant announced at the end of each day, and he would add the number of miles gained.

In camp Sven helped Dillon brush and clean the mules, feed them and lead them to water. He tried to relieve their pain by covering their sores with mud. With Billy he gathered wood and tended the campfire each evening and morning.

During the day he led one or two of the mules. As the soldiers built the corduroy paths the times necessary to pull the mules from the mud lessened. Their loads lightened as the soldiers ate the food they carried.

"Corporal Young, tomorrow morning take Ayres and

Evans and two mules and go back for supplies," Lieutenant Castner ordered the evening of their fifth day of trail cutting. "Sven, join me in my tent."

"Yes, Sir." He followed Lt. Castner. "These are my last two pieces of smoked salmon." The lieutenant handed one to Sven and took a bite from the other.

"I am sending you ahead with Hicks and Billy tomorrow. With two mules gone, Dillon does not need help. Hicks will lead you to a stream. Think you can catch some fish?"

"I hope so, Sir."

"I hope so too. Get a good night's sleep."

13

"BILLY, Sven, let's go," Mr. Hicks called as the boys ate breakfast. "Sven, do you have your fishing pole?"

"String and hook," Sven said. "I'll make a pole."

"Follow me."

Sven and Billy followed the guide from camp. With two swings of his hatchet, Mr. Hicks blazed a mark on each side of a tree.

"Why are you marking both sides?" Sven asked. "Lieutenant Castner only blazes one side."

"I have to return."

Sven nodded.

"We go far?" Billy asked.

Mr. Hicks shrugged. "Until we find a place to catch fish. You stay with Sven today and cook fish for the soldiers to eat. Now quit talking and walk faster."

He increased his pace. "One, two, three ... twelve," He counted his steps to the next large tree. Slash. Slash. "One, two, three ... ten." Slash. Slash.

"Here," Mr. Hicks said. After a long hike he stopped on the bank of a shallow stream. "We will camp here tonight."

"Where are soldiers?" Billy asked.

"They are following us, cutting trail," Mr. Hicks replied. "You make a clearing for the tents." He handed Billy his hatchet. "Then light a fire."

"What Sven do?"

"Sven is going to catch fish for our evening meal."

"Billy fish?"

"No, you clear a place for the tents and start a fire," Mr. Hicks repeated. "I will see you boys this evening."

"Where you go?" Billy asked.

"I am going to help the soldiers." Mr. Hicks hiked away in the direction they had come.

Sven cut a long willow stem and trimmed it. He notched the end and tied his string to it. He fastened a snip of red cloth, ripped from his kerchief, to his hook.

"Billy fish?" the native youth asked him.

"No, cut a clearing and light a fire," Sven said. "Let me show you." He took the hatchet from Billy.

He blazed one side from a circle of trees. "Cut down everything except large trees within this circle. Cut the brush and small trees down to the ground like the soldiers do."

Sven chopped a sapling tree off level with the ground. "Save the wood for our fire."

"Billy fish," Billy said when Sven handed him the hatchet.

"Clear out the brush and light a fire," Sven said.

When Billy began chopping, Sven walked upstream and looked for a good fishing spot. He fished in three likely looking pools but did not get a nibble.

"Ha-ee-yah!"

Billy's shout scared Sven as he hiked farther upstream. With fishing line trailing, he ran. Where the clearing should have been, there was no clearing and no Billy.

"Billy, where are you?" Sven shouted.

"Billy fish."

Sven hurried downstream. He found Billy standing at the river's edge, holding a long pointed stick. Near Billy's feet lay a large fish.

"Billy make trap." Billy pointed toward a row of sticks stuck upright in the river, angled downstream.

Sven saw a fish swimming upstream, being forced toward shore by Billy's row of sticks.

Billy speared the fish with his pointed stick. "Trout," He said and laid the fish by the other. "Billy fish."

"All right, Billy, you fish," Sven said and smiled. "Give me the hatchet."

Sven chopped down the shrubs and small trees and lit the fire. He cut off the heads and cleaned the trout that Billy speared.

That evening, after Mr. Hicks led the soldiers into camp, Sven roasted the fish.

"Good work, Billy," Mr. Hicks said and patted Billy on the back. "You cleared a good place for the tents."

Billy smiled and said, "Billy fish. Sven chop clearing."

"I wasn't catching any fish," Sven explained. "Billy made a trap which funneled fish to shore where he speared them. Thank Billy for the trout we have to eat."

After the soldiers set up their tents, Sven served trout. "There wasn't enough to smoke any," he whispered in Lt. Castner's ear.

"Try again tomorrow," Lt. Castner said. He took a bite and smiled. "This is delicious."

The smile turned into a frown when Powers asked, "Why are we cutting this trail, Lieutenant? Nobody is going to use it. Too many mosquitoes."

"Let's quit, Lieutenant," VanSchoonhoven said, "while we still have blood." He swatted a mosquito on his forehead and waved his hand to chase away those on his food. "Shoo."

"I agree," Woodruff said. "Look at those poor animals. They're being eaten alive. It is no wonder that we have to pull them out of mudholes and up every hill."

"Don't be discouraged, Men. We will make it," Lt. Castner said. "We are making excellent progress, so don't give up. Sven, take care of the mules."

Sven led the mules and horse to the river to drink. He packed mud on their pus-running sores. "You have the worst of it," he said quietly. "I hope this mud helps."

As Sven hobbled the mules, Billy ran into the clearing.

"Bears, Two bears," Billy screamed. "Billy check trap. Bears eat fish."

89

"Now will we turn back, Lieutenant?" VanSchoonhoven asked. "Bears will eat us faster than mosquitoes do."

Lt. Castner laughed. "Nobody is going to be eaten, but to be safe, we will have guards tonight. We don't want bears eating our animals or food. Powers, you take the first two hours. Woodruff, second two. Dillinger, third. VanSchoonhoven, fourth. Fire into the air if you see a bear."

Sven fell asleep as he listened to Powers on guard duty, singing softly to himself.

———

BANG!

Sven popped up from his blanket and dressed quickly.

"Where's the bear?" He heard Lt. Castner ask. "Van, where is the bear?"

Sven crawled from the tent.

"I didn't see it," VanSchoonhoven said, "I heard it growl."

"Look around, Men," Lt. Castner said. "If you see bears scare them away or shoot them."

"No bear, Lieutenant," McGregor reported when he returned to the clearing. "I saw a cow moose with its calf across the river."

"Hear that, VanSchoonhoven?" Lt. Castner asked. "It's a moose. Since you woke us up early, we'll get an early start. We'll camp here again tonight."

Sven and Billy stayed in camp as the men extended the trail across the stream. Billy speared more fish which Sven cut into strips and smoked.

———

Cpl. Young returned from Knik with supplies that evening.

"Is this all you have?" Lt. Castner asked as he looked at the food being unloaded from the two mules.

Cpl. Young nodded. "We ate some on the trail."

"That's not fair, Lieutenant," VanSchoonhoven said. "We did the work and they ate the best food."

"Quit complaining; it doesn't help," Lt. Castner said. "From now on, whoever goes for supplies, remember the ones here doing the hard work. They need the food more than you do on the trail."

Lt. Castner entered his tent as the men grumbled about the lack of food.

Sven followed the lieutenant. "Sir, may I come in?"

"Enter, Sven."

"Thank you, Sir," He handed the lieutenant a small package. "I smoked some fish for you today."

"Thank you, Sven."

"And I was wondering, Sir. Each evening you praise the men and tell them how fast we are going. When will we get to Circle City?"

"We have a long way to go," Lt. Castner said as, deep in thought, he stroked his chin. "I did not realize how difficult it would be. The soft ground and mud are the big problems. Getting supplies will be a problem as we get farther from Cook Inlet. It will be August before we get to Circle City?"

"I lost track of time, Sir," Sven said. "What day is it?"

Lt. Castner smiled. "It is hard to keep track of time. My chronometers help me." He opened a case and Sven saw an instrument that showed both time and date. "It's June 19, almost the longest day of the year. We should be in Circle City by August 20. How does that sound?"

"Good, Sir. Where is Circle City?"

Lt. Castner unfolded a map and pointed. "We're here; we'll call this Moose Creek. We continue this way and cross the mountains and then we're there." He traced a route on the map with his finger.

Sven nodded. "One more question, Sir. Why do the soldiers complain so much?"

"That's the way soldiers are, and most people, too. If everything is not the way they think it should be, they complain. They don't like mud. They don't like mosquitoes. They don't like hard work. They don't like the weather. You, Sven, are determined to get to Circle City to find your father, so you don't complain."

"Yes, Sir."

"I must to get to Circle City because that is what I am ordered to do. I am determined to obey my orders and develop a trail there. That is why I praise the soldiers even if they don't work hard. If you and I can make them more cheerful, they will work harder."

"Yes, Sir."

The lieutenant took a piece of smoked fish and handed the package to Sven. "Give each man a piece. It may improve their spirit."

14

"STUPID mule," Dillon yelled as the mule he led slipped and fell into Moose Creek. He kicked the mule and left it.

"Don't do that." Sven ran to the fallen mule. "Come on, Molly, you can make it. Get up."

He gently tugged at the lead rope, and Molly struggled to her feet and limped up the bank. Blood streamed from a cut in its left foreleg.

"Lieutenant," Dillon called. "This mule is done for. Should I shoot it?"

"Don't kill it," Sven protested.

Lt. Castner looked at the cut leg. "Wrap up the leg, Dillon. We need the mule. Give it a couple of days' rest."

"Yes, Sir," Dillon said. "Sven, help me here. You will be in charge of this mule until it heals. Get something to wrap the leg."

Sven ran to Pvt. VanSchoonhoven. "Van, I need a bandage."

"What for?" VanSchoonhoven scowled.

"Molly. She cut her leg."

"My bandages are for the soldiers, not for an ornery mule."

"Do you want to carry more in your pack?" Sven asked. "If the mule dies, you carry more."

"What we should do," VanSchoonhoven said, "is turn

around and go back to Washington. I'm tired of mud and mosquitoes and chopping down trees. I'm trained to be a medic. I'm in the hospital corps."

"I know," Sven said. "Here's a chance to help a mule and help yourself. We are not going back, so bandage the mule's leg or carry what it is carrying. Come on."

"Don't tell me what to do, Boy. I am not a veterinarian." VanSchoonhoven grumbled; but he followed Sven and bandaged the mule's leg.

Sven tended the limping mule as he followed the trail cutters. In the early afternoon he helped Dillon clear an area for a new camp and set up the tents.

In the evening the soldiers, who worked in pairs, straggled wearily into camp. VanSchoonhoven returned by himself. As he ate his evening meal, he sat alone and muttered.

"Do you have a problem, Van?" Lt. Castner asked when he heard him.

"Hicks and Billy."

"Where are they?"

"I don't know," VanSchoonhoven said. "We were cutting brush together and they disappeared. I came back to camp 'cause I thought they would be here."

"You know you are supposed to stay together."

"I know. Tell them."

"I'll find out what happened when Hicks returns," Lt. Castner said. "Get some sleep."

Sven lay awake, listening to the snoring of his tent mates, when Mr. Hicks and Billy returned to camp.

"It's almost midnight. Where have you been?" he heard Lt. Castner ask.

"Cutting trail," Mr. Hicks replied. "Where's VanSchoonhoven? Is he here?"

"Asleep."

"He deserted us, said he had to pee."

"That's not what he said," Lt. Castner said. "I'll deal with him in the morning."

———

As he assigned his men their work the next morning, Lt. Castner singled out VanSchoonhoven. "Van, you need to improve your attitude. Hicks tells me you deserted him yesterday. You work with Dillon and Sven today. Clean up here, pack the tents, load the mules, and help set up a new camp later. Dillon is in charge."

"I don't take orders from civilians," muttered Van-Schoonhoven, "not from Hicks yesterday, not from Dillon."

"What did you say?" Lt. Castner clenched his fists as he glared at VanSchoonhoven.

"I said ..."

"I heard what you said. You would be wise to stop complaining and obey orders. Drat it all, I have had enough of your bad attitude."

"We ought to turn around and go back."

"Get that idea out of your head. Do you understand?" Lt. Castner ordered.

"Yes, Sir,"

"Good. Now get to work." Lt. Castner stalked away.

"Lieutenant's got no sense," VanSchoonhoven muttered as he helped Sven fold a tent.

"I couldn't help hearing you argue with Lieutenant Castner," Sven said. "Complaining doesn't help. It makes the lieutenant angry. You know he is not going back so why ..."

"I don't need you telling me anything," VanSchoonhoven interrupted Sven. "I don't know why we keep a baby-faced boy around. You shouldn't be here. We don't need you receiving special favors and eating our food."

Sven shrugged his shoulders and rubbed his smooth chin. Only Billy and he, and Lt. Castner, who shaved every morning, were not growing beards, and the lieutenant kept a moustache. Sven felt the soft peach fuzz whiskers under his own nose.

VanSchoonhoven sullenly did what Dillon ordered and nothing more. Sven did his usual work and thought how Dillon and he usually accomplished cheerfully what the three of them now did unhappily. Lt. Castner had left them with his problem.

———

In the evening the next day, VanSchoonhoven handed a smashed chronometer to Lt. Castner. "Ornery mule stepped on it."

Lt. Castner's fist clenched as he inspected the useless time keeping instrument. "Drat it all, Van, how did it happen?"

"It fell from the pack."

"Dillon, Sven, did either of you see this happen?" Lt. Castner held up the broken instrument.

"No, Sir," Dillon answered.

To Sven it looked as if someone had smashed it with an axe. "No, Sir," he said. "How will you know what day it is now?"

"If we don't know what day it is," VanSchoonhoven said, "maybe we should turn back now, before it is too late."

"I have my own chronometer," Lt. Castner said and scowled at VanSchoonhoven. "You should know by now that we are not turning back. Sven. I want to talk to you."

"Yes, Sir." He followed the lieutenant into his tent.

"Did you see the chronometer fall or the mule step on it?"

"No, Sir."

"Did you see Van smash it?"

"No, Sir, but I try to stay away from him. Dillon and I both do. All he does is complain. Why did you leave him with us?"

"Because no one else likes to work with him, either," Lt. Castner said. "If he wasn't our medic I would send him back to Captain Glenn. Keep an eye on him, Sven, so he doesn't do more damage."

"Yes, Sir."

Sven watched VanSchoonhoven the next day but observed nothing unusual. The private complained and did only what Dillon commanded him to do.

————

Sven wondered if he had failed in his spying that evening when he discovered that the mules and horse were gone.

"Dillon," he yelled, "come quick. The animals got loose."

Dillon, Lt. Castner, and everyone except VanSchoonhoven ran to where the animals had been tethered.

"I came to move them to a new spot to get fresh grass," Sven said, "and they're gone."

"Dillon, you'd better find those animals," Lt. Castner said. "Powers, you go with him. Sven, come with me."

Sven followed the lieutenant into his tent.

"Did Van have anything to do with the animals getting loose? I noticed he didn't come to see what had happened."

"I don't think so, Sir." Sven said. "I watched him all day."

"Who tied up the animals?"

"I think Dillon did. He does it all the time."

"Thanks, Sven. That's all." He patted Sven on the back. "I wish my men were as anxious to reach Circle City as you are."

Sven smiled as he sat at the campfire and listened to the men grumble. He watched VanSchoonhoven who, for a change, smiled and seemed to enjoy himself.

He saw VanSchoonhoven's smile turn into a scowl when, about two hours later, Dillon and Powers returned with all five animals.

"I can't believe it," Dillon said. "Don't know how those animals could get so far away so quick. Must have been three or four miles. Good thing they left a good trail."

"Good thing they were all on the same tether line," Powers said, "or we would still be looking."

"And it's a good thing we have them back," Lt. Castner

said. "I can't imagine what we would have done without them. You men would have had to carry heavy packs."

———

The next morning, Lt. Castner, gave new orders. "Corporal Young, you, Dillon, and Powers take two mules and go for more supplies. McGregor, you work with Sven as camp manager until Dillon returns. VanSchoonhoven, you will work with me. I don't want to hear any complaining. Do you understand?"

"Yes, Sir." VanSchoonhoven scowled as he replied.

———

The next few days Sven enjoyed working with his friend. A test of his skill with animals came when McGregor and he caught up with the trail cutters at Chickaloon Creek at noon on June twenty-ninth.

The men had felled several large trees and were trying to position them as a bridge across the swiftly flowing stream. The water pushed the loose ends of the logs back toward the bank.

"Glad you're here," Lt. Castner said. "We can use the mules to tow the logs into position on the other side. Come on, Sven."

They tied the mules, with their packs off, to the free ends of the logs to pull them to the far bank. Sven and Lt. Castner each rode a blindfolded mule into the stream.

"It's not working," Sven yelled as the current pushed against the mules and the logs. The powerful current swept them downstream.

15

"Ow," Sven yelled as Lt. Castner's mule crashed into him. He urged Molly, the mule he rode, forward.

But mule and rider were helpless. The strong current swung the logs, tied to shore at one end, back toward the bank. To avoid being crushed between the two mules, Sven slide from Molly's back into the icy water. He kept a tight grip on Molly's harness.

"Cut the rope," Lt. Castner yelled.

Water rushed over Sven's head as he reached for the knife in his boot top. As water rushed over him, he hacked through the rope until it snapped. He pulled himself onto Molly's back as the current carried them downstream.

"Come on, Molly. You can make it." he urged the terrified mule to the far shore.

"Why don't we make a raft for our supplies?" Sven asked after he rejoined Lt. Castner. "I'll ride back to the other side so the men can ride across."

Lt. Castner nodded. "Try it. The bridge won't work. Have three men build a raft. Bring the others across on the mules to cut the trail. I'll hike ahead and blaze the route."

"Yes, Sir."

Riding one mule and leading the other, Sven recrossed Chickaloon Creek.

"McGregor, Evans, Dillinger, build a raft. Lieutenant

Castner's orders," Sven said. "The rest of you get your axes and saws. You're to cut trail as soon as I get you across. Ayres and VanSchoonhoven, get on the mules."

"Why must I obey you?" VanSchoonhoven asked. "You don't even belong here."

"Because the lieutenant said so, Van," McGregor said, "and you're in enough trouble with him."

Sven smiled and said nothing. He rode the horse and led the mules, carrying VanSchoonhoven and Ayres, into the stream. With another trip he had all but the raft builders across.

When the raft was completed, Sven had the soldiers tie ropes to each end. "Evans and Dillinger stay here. Snub the rope around that tree and let it out as McGregor and I pull the raft to the other side. Come on, Mac. We'll ride the mules." He picked up the end of the other rope and carried it as he and McGregor crossed the stream.

"Stay up, Mac." Sven jumped to the ground, picked up a sturdy branch and tied the rope to it.

Climbing back on his mule, Sven handed one end of the branch to McGregor. "Hold it in front of you."

He waved to Evans and Dillinger. "Now, Mac. Get up, mules."

As the mules walked side by side, they towed the loaded raft across Chickaloon Creek and onto the bank.

"Good work," Sven said, "I'll go back for Evans and Dillinger."

"Leave the ropes tied to the raft," McGregor said. "Corporal Young can use it when he comes with our supplies."

Safely across the river, they rubbed down and brushed the wet, weary mules and horse.

As they worked McGregor asked, "Sven, where did you learn to use mules like that?"

"You learn a lot working on a farm," Sven replied. "We used mules to pull out stumps and drag logs. They're strong animals."

With tents and gear and their meager food supply reloaded on the mules, they hurried forward to help cut trail.

After setting up camp the following evening, Lt. Castner said, "We will take tomorrow off. Our rations are low; all we have left are bacon and tea, so we will wait for supplies to catch up with us. Perhaps Mac and Sven can catch some fish."

"Why don't Billy and I shoot a sheep?" Mr. Hicks asked. "We saw some on the mountain yesterday."

"That would certainly help," Lt. Castner said. "Take Woodruff with you; he's our best sharpshooter."

After a meager breakfast of bacon and tea, Sven and McGregor hiked back to Chickaloon Creek. With nothing but snips of Sven's red kerchief to attract the fish, they caught only three small trout.

"It's useless," McGregor said. "We'd better go back to camp."

"Not before I try something else," Sven said. "This reminds me of the stream at Hope. Maybe there is gold."

He pulled his pan from his backpack, scooped gravel from the stream bed and swished water through it.

"Look, Mac." Three flecks of gold remained in his pan. "Gold."

After McGregor looked, Sven turned the pan over and let the gold flecks fall into the stream.

"So, why don't you keep it?" McGregor asked.

"No place to carry it. If I find any nuggets I'll keep them."

Sven scooped up more gravel. Each pan contained a few flecks which he dumped out.

"If that is all you are doing, Sven, let's go," McGregor said. "I'm getting hungry."

"One more pan," Sven said. "There's no food so we don't have to rush." He swished water through the gravel in his pan.

A nugget the size of his finger tip lay in the bottom of the pan. He glanced at McGregor who was picking up his pack, and slipped the nugget into his pocket. Later he would add it to those in his pouch.

"No nuggets, Mac," he lied as he dumped two flecks of gold back into the stream.

They hiked to camp and shared bits of their three fish among nine people at the evening meal. The hunters had shot no sheep.

The following afternoon Cpl. Young arrived with their food supply, but the men on the trail had eaten the best food.

"This is not good," Lt. Castner announced after questioning Cpl. Young. "To save our food supply I must send some of you back. Evans, Powers, Dillinger, pack up and return to Knik. Report to Captain Glenn."

"Yes, Sir," the three men responded happily.

"Let me go back," VanSchoonhoven said. "I hate cutting trail. I hate mosquitoes."

"I can't let you go, Van," Lt. Castner said. "You are our medic so you have to stay, all the way to Circle City."

VanSchoonhoven glared at Lt. Castner. Under his breath he muttered, "Not if I can help it. I'll do what I can so we all go back."

"I heard that!" Lt. Castner snapped as he clinched his fists. "Bread and water for you for two weeks. Not you or anyone else will stop us."

Sven, pleased that Lt. Castner remained determined to reach Circle City, smiled, but he wondered about keeping VanSchoonhoven on bread and water. There was not enough food for any of them for two weeks.

Their food supply increased when Mr. Hicks, Billy, and Woodruff shot four bighorn sheep. They would eat well for a few days.

"Looks like I am just on time for dinner."

Sven whirled around from the fire where Mac and he were roasting the leg of a sheep. A tall stranger walked toward them.

"Who are you?" Lt. Castner asked as he stepped from his tent.

"Luther Kelly. I'm a guide. Captain Glenn sent me to join you."

"I'm not sure you are welcome." Lt. Castner frowned as he stroked his chin. "I don't have much to offer you. Short rations and hard work are all we have."

"It looks like you have plenty to eat."

"That's about the last of our meat, and we have little else." With another person in camp and his men on half rations, Lt. Castner feared that the food would not feed them all.

———

The next morning, when only mutton, dried apples, and tea remained, Lt. Castner called the men together.

"VanSchoonhoven," he said, "you are going to get your wish. All of you soldiers are going back to our supply camp. Corporal Young, you are in charge. Dillon will go with you. Take all the mules and return here with one or two of the men and all the supplies you can. Is that clear?"

"Yes, Sir."

"Those not returning here, report to Captain Glenn. Is that clear?"

"Yes, Sir," the privates answered together.

"We will camp here until you return with supplies. Now get your gear together and leave. Corporal Young, I will expect you back here by the twenty-fourth."

"Yes, Sir."

"Lieutenant Castner," Sven asked after the soldiers departed, "we're not going to reach Circle City by mid-August, are we?"

"We will see, Sven. It will probably be the first of September. We will cut trail while we wait for our supplies."

Sven worked with Lt. Castner, the two guides, and Billy. They cut brush and felled trees each day and returned to what they called Sheep Camp each evening.

Daily rain made their work difficult. Sven tried wearing his slicker but it hindered his movement. Like the others he let the rain soak his clothes.

"I hope Corporal Young arrives soon with our supplies," Lt. Castner said more than once, as they chopped shrubs down. "I am afraid that rain might make it impossible. I hope he can get through the swamps and rivers."

"What do we do if he doesn't get here?" Sven asked.

Lt. Castner shrugged hopelessly and said, "He has to come."

———

The evening of July twenty-four, the day Lt. Castner had ordered him to return, Cpl. Young, with Dillon and McGregor, two mules and the horse, arrived.

"Are we glad to see you," Lt. Castner greeted the three men. "You look loaded down."

"About eight hundred pounds of food," Cpl. Young said. "We ate little on the trail."

"That's good. We can travel to Circle City with that much food," Lt. Castner said and smiled for the first time in several days. "We should be there by early September. What orders did you receive from Captain Glenn?"

"He did not give me any orders." Cpl. Young said.

"No orders? Then we will follow those I have. Tomorrow we will rest the mules and horse and prepare to leave."

"I'm going back to Knik," Luther Kelly said. "I don't want to be a reason for your running short of supplies. I'll tell Captain Glenn where you are heading."

"I appreciate that; thank you," Lt. Castner said.

"How about you, Sven," the lieutenant teased, "do you want to go back? We still have a long way to go."

"Me? I'm going with you, Sir. I will celebrate my September birthday with my father in Circle City."

16

SVEN, like the others remaining with Lt. Castner, carried his blankets, extra clothes, and eating utensils in his pack. The horse and mules carried the food, except up hills.

"Dratted good-for-nothing mules." Dillon swore each time they unloaded the animals and carried the packs uphill. "I wish you bags of bones would die so I could go back."

Sven bit his lip. He had promised Lt. Castner that he would not complain. "Don't you want to get to Circle City, Dillon? We won't make it without them."

"I don't think we'll make it with them."

As they ate breakfast the morning after a particularly difficult day, Dillon said, "Lieutenant, I'm not sure the mules will last much longer. We should go back."

"Nonsense, Dillon." Lt. Castner said. "We are making excellent progress. Look ahead. With that open ground in front of us, we will move faster. Sven and I will go ahead today to mark a trail. I will try to make it easier for the animals."

As Lt. Castner paced off the miles, Sven blazed the trail.

He slashed small trees or axed the tops off shrub plants so the others could follow.

As Sven slashed a tree, Lt. Castner called softly, "Look."

A short distance ahead stood a native man, watching them.

"Raise your hand," Lt. Castner said.

Using the greeting Billy had taught them, Lt. Castner and Sven raised their hands, open palms forward. The native raised his hand.

"Sven, run back and get Billy. We need our interpreter."

Sven dropped his pack and ran back along the trail.

"We met a native," he called when he approached the others. "Billy, come with me. Lieutenant Castner needs you. Hurry."

The two youth ran forward.

"Billy, find out who this man is," Lt. Castner said as they joined him.

Sven listened as Billy spoke to the man in their Athabascan language.

"He is Matanuska chief," Billy interpreted. "Name is Andre. He say come to camp."

"Tell him we will be happy to visit," Lt. Castner said.

When Cpl. Young, Mr. Hicks, Dillon, and McGregor joined them, they followed Chief Andre to his camp on the shore of a small lake. The native men, women, and children, all talking at once, crowded around them.

Sven smiled at the children who gathered around him. A few reached out and touched his hands and one bold boy touched his cheek.

"Billy, what are they doing?" he asked.

"They surprised. Never see white skin man before."

The natives stared as Chief Andre ate a meal of fish with Lt. Castner and his men.

"Tell the chief we will camp nearby," Lt. Castner told Billy after the meal. "Tell him I need men to carry packs for us and that we will pay them. Dillon, if we hire natives you may get your wish to take the mules back to Knik."

"I hope so," Dillon said.

"Billy, invite all the natives to our camp in the morning," Lt. Castner said.

———

In the morning Sven helped serve tea and sugar to all the natives, and he distributed needles as gifts to the women.

As the natives drank their tea, Chief Andre scowled and spoke angrily with his men.

"What's the matter, Billy?" Lt. Castner asked. "Doesn't the chief like tea?"

"Chief Andre say you bad man. Chief not eat first, then men. Women and children not eat last."

"Tell Chief Andre I am sorry," Lt. Castner said. "I did not know their custom. Sven, offer the chief more sugar."

Chief Andre slapped the sugar from Sven's hand and glared at Lt. Castner. After angry words and a gesture, he led his people back toward their camp.

One man turned back and talked to Billy.

"Lieutenant. Man say he carry pack."

"One packer is not enough," Lt. Castner said, "but tell him if he will carry sixty pounds he will be paid two dollars a day. I am sorry, Men. I should have asked about their customs. We aren't welcome anymore. Get ready to move."

"Lieutenant," Mr. Hicks said, "I am going back to Knik. I've gone farther than I have ever gone before. We all should go back. Winter is coming and I don't think you will get to Circle City."

Sven frowned as he wondered if they would turn back or continue on without a guide.

"I am sorry you feel that way, Hicks," Lt. Castner said. "I can't keep you from leaving, and we'll miss you. Corporal Young, return with Hicks and report to Captain Glenn that I am continuing on to Circle City."

"Yes, Sir."

"Billy, I want you to stay to be my interpreter. Will you go with us?"

"Yes, Sir." Billy snapped to attention and saluted.

Sven smiled. Billy imitated the regular soldiers just as he did himself. He sighed in relief; before long he would be in Circle City.

As Cpl. Young and Mr. Hicks departed to the south, Lt. Castner led the way north. They stopped in less than a mile when Chief Andre stepped out of the woods. The chief waved his arms about him, shivered and shook, and performed a weird pantomime.

Sven, along with Lt. Castner, Dillon, and McGregor, laughed at the chief's antics. Billy and the Matanuskan native did not laugh.

"No laugh," Billy said. "Chief Andre say snow in one month. White men freeze."

"We will be in Circle City in one month," Lt. Castner said.

To Sven it seemed that they would soon reach their destination. In ten days, traveling on hard, dry ground, they traveled more miles that they had in six weeks of cutting trail.

As Sven anticipated finding his father, he often asked Lt. Castner the same questions. "What day is it? How much farther? When will we get there?"

"My maps show 200 miles. If we travel ten miles a day, we should be their in twenty days," Lt. Castner answered one day. "I hoped we could travel more easily as we climbed higher. I thought the ground would be hard and I did not expect these lakes and swamps. It should be easier to travel as we get higher up the mountains."

The lieutenant led toward a pass in the Alaska Mountain Range. On sunny days they traveled straight north except for detours around swamps and lakes. On cloudy, rainy days they used an unreliable compass or guesswork, and hiked northward.

Sven walked ahead with Lt. Castner or led the mule, Kid, urging it onward. When the other mule and the horse bogged down and had to be unloaded, Sven coaxed Kid forward.

"I don't know how you do it, Sven," Dillon said one evening. "You sure have a knack with that mule. What's your secret?"

"It's no secret," Sven said and smiled. "Kind words and gentleness work better than slaps and swearing."

———

One evening, as Sven helped himself to a second serving of beans, Lt. Castner said, "We have good appetites. It must be the fresh air and hard work, and for Sven it may be because he is a fast growing young man. But I have bad news; I am afraid that we will run out of food before we reach Circle City. We will ration our supplies; less food for everyone and no second helpings. If we see animals we will shoot them."

———

Two days later, the Matanuskan pack carrier spotted five swans on a small lake. Lt. Castner ordered him and Billy to circle the lake, one from each direction.

"Sven, come with me," Lt. Castner said. "When they drive the swans in our direction we will shoot them." He handed Sven a shotgun. "Ever use one of these?"

"Yes, Sir. I hunted quail in Minnesota."

"Good, then you know what to do."

Sven and Lt. Castner crouched in tangled shrubs as the swans swam toward them.

"Wait until they are near shore," Lt. Castner whispered. "We don't want to swim after them. You shoot the one on the far left. I'll shoot the one on the right. ... What's that?"

Wild thrashing through the brush frightened the swans and they swam back toward the center of the lake. Sven stood up with his gun ready to shoot. He saw Billy, wide-eyed, scrambling toward camp.

"It's Billy. Something scared him."

"Let's go back," Lt. Castner said and sighed. "Roast swam would have been delicious." He signaled for the Matanuskan to follow them.

Sven put an arm over Billy's shoulder when he found him hunched up, shivering before the campfire.

"What happened, Billy? Did you see a bear?" Lt. Castner asked.

"Bigfoot," Billy said. "Bigfoot no take Billy."

"Did you see Bigfoot?"

"No. Billy remember. Bigfoot take person alone."

"There is no Bigfoot," Lt. Castner said, "and we have no swans to eat."

"I am glad you are all right, Billy, and that Bigfoot did not take you." Sven squeezed Billy's shoulder. "I will stay with you so Bigfoot does not get either of us."

17

"Sven, I don't think you should have promised to let Billy stay close to you," Lt. Castner said the next morning, "He refuses to stay with Dillon and Mac to help with the animals. You will have to stay and Mac will lead with me."

"Yes, Sir," Sven replied. "I don't mind, not if it helps Billy. My mother said I should keep my promises."

"Your mother is a wise woman," the lieutenant said. "I cannot imagine why you ran away."

Sven turned away as tears trickled down his cheeks. Each time someone mentioned his mother he became homesick, and he thought about how wrong he had been to leave. Only the thought of finding his father kept him determined to reach Circle City.

With Billy as his companion, he lead the mule Kid and plodded along behind Dillon and the Matanuskan pack carrier. After two days of trudging they reached the high mountain pass.

"I have good news and bad news, Men," Lt. Castner said as he studied his maps that evening. "The good news is that it is not far to Circle City."

"What is the bad news?" Dillon asked.

"We are using our food faster than I anticipated. From now on we will live on half rations."

"That is bad," Dillon said. "I am hungry all the time now, and I can't imagine how these animals feel. There isn't much here for them to eat."

"I'm sorry, Dillon," Lt. Castner said. "We are all hungry and could use double rations. Tighten your belts. Get a good night's sleep. We will put in longer days and get to Circle City more quickly."

An early start the next morning did not help. That afternoon the mule Fanny stumbled and fell.

"Stupid, no-good mule, get up." Dillon tugged on Fanny's rope and swore. "Wait here. I'll fetch the lieutenant."

With Dillon gone, Sven talked softly to the mule but it would not get back on its feet.

"Should I shoot it?" Dillon asked when he returned.

"No, we need Fanny to carry supplies," Lt. Castner said. "Set up camp here."

"Look!" Billy yelled and pointed as they set up their tents. A native man and boy walked toward them.

"Find out who they are, Billy," Lt. Castner ordered.

After a short conversation, Billy reported. "Man and son from Copper River. Hunt caribou."

"Ask the man if he will carry supplies to the Tanana River for us," Lt. Castner said.

Billy and the man gestured and argued, until Billy grinned and said, "He say carry supplies."

"Good. Maybe we will shoot Fanny," Lt. Castner said.

"Now?" asked Dillon.

"Don't, please," Sven said. "Let me try to get her up."

In his pan he carried water from a pond, held Fanny's head and poured water into her mouth. He pulled grass from the few small clumps that grew at that high altitude. Fanny chewed but did not rise.

"Go to bed, Sven," Lt. Castner ordered. "You did all you could."

Sven crawled into his tent and lay next to Billy. He

fell asleep as he worried that Fanny would be shot in the morning.

———

He arose early to try one more time to save Fanny. The mule was not there.

"She's up!" Sven shouted when he saw Fanny nibbling on some grass near the pond. "Fanny's up."

His shouts awakened the others.

"Then let's get going," Lt. Castner said as he stepped from his tent. "Everybody up. Let's eat and be on our way."

They hurried onward. In the high alpine meadow of the pass the air was cold. Snow covered the peaks around them. They had no time to waste.

"Look!" Lt. Castner shouted when those with the supplies stopped where he waited. He pointed at a small rivulet.

"What's so exciting about that?" Dillon asked.

"It's flowing north!" Lt. Castner said and laughed. "It is downhill from here."

Sven smiled. He could not remember seeing the lieutenant so happy. "How many more days to Circle City?"

"Two weeks, Sven. Two weeks," Lt. Castner said. "It's August sixteen. We will be there September first."

"He say, 'Tanana River two sleeps,'" Billy said and pointed to their Matanuskan pack carrier.

"That is good news," Lt. Castner said. "Let's go."

———

But two sleeps later snow swirled around them as they hiked through the high mountain pass. Ice crusted the ponds and small lakes. The snow turned to rain as they descended beside the stream to a lower elevation.

Sven, wearing his badly worn Mackinaw and torn slicker, did not complain. His clothes kept him warmer and drier than those worn by his companions.

As they walked, hunched against the rain and cold, Billy grabbed Sven's arm and pointed. Two hundred yards away a native man walked parallel to them.

"Bad," Billy said. "His hunting ground."

"Lieutenant Castner," Sven shouted.

When the lieutenant stopped, Sven pointed to the man.

"Billy, ask him into camp," Lt. Castner ordered.

"Come." Billy tugged Sven's arm and the two walked toward the man.

Billy called to the man, who stopped and yelled back to him.

"Don't know what he say," Billy said. "He talk different."

"Use your hand signs," Sven said.

With gestures Billy invited the man to follow. Through gesturing, Lt. Castner hired him to carry supplies.

"Copper River man leave," Billy told Lt. Castner as the man and his son left camp. "He afraid. Not his hunting ground."

Lt. Castner looked at the departing natives and sighed. "Gain one, lose one. Let's go."

The lieutenant led northward, downhill and downstream. It rained every day. Crossing streams and small glaciers tired the half-starved men and boys.

One day they stopped at a camp of friendly natives. After gesturing with Lt. Castner, the natives shared dried salmon with them.

Lt. Castner did not allow his men time to enjoy the treat. "We need to hurry, Men. Eat as you walk," he ordered.

They hurried during the day, camped as it became dark, and started again at the first light of dawn. They hurried until Fanny refused to climb a hill.

Dillon tried to move Fanny with blows and kicks and swearing. Sven spoke softly but without success.

After two hours Lt. Castner ordered, "Shoot her and butcher her. We will eat her meat. Since she won't carry supplies, she can help feed us."

Sven turned away and he held his ears as Dillon shot Fanny. Tears welled up in his eyes.

"What matter, Sven?" Billy asked as he laid his hand on Sven's shoulder. "You sad?"

"I hate to see animals die, Billy. Fanny worked hard and now she is dead."

"We need eat," Billy said. "Good meat."

When they heard a second shot, farther away, he exclaimed, "We eat much good!"

"Why? What was that?" Sven asked.

"Matanuskan, other man, shoot sheep." Billy pointed across the valley toward the two natives.

———

Sven felt better the next morning as they left camp with full stomachs. He led their last mule, Kid, and Dillon lead the horse along a narrow animal trail beside the river.

"No!" Dillon screamed and swore as the horse stumbled and rolled into the icy water. "Help!"

Sven scrambled down the bank and held the horse's head out of the water. Dillon, Lt. Castner, McGregor, and he struggled in their attempt to pull the heavy animal from the river.

"It's no use," Lt. Castner said as they rested. "We can't do it."

"Better shoot it," Dillon said. "It will drown if Sven lets its head down."

"Do it," Lt. Castner ordered. "Come along, Sven. I know you don't want to watch and neither do I."

Leaving the shooting to Dillon and McGregor, they climbed the bank.

As the shot echoed up from the river, Lt. Castner swore, "Drat it all. Where are our packers? Why did we leave them alone?"

"Billy! Billy!" Sven called. "Billy wouldn't run away."

"Looks like he has," Lt. Castner said. "They've taken a tent, food, and who knows what else."

"It looks like the rest of our trip is up to us and Kid," the lieutenant said when Dillon and McGregor joined them. "We have been deserted."

With their food almost gone, clothes in rags, and, except for Sven, footwear tied together with straps from discarded pack saddles, they trudged beside the river.

The four crowded together to sleep in the lieutenant's tent that evening.

As he wrote his daily report, Lt. Castner tried to be cheerful and said, "By my counting we have come 298 miles from our base camp. We are all weak, but we can get to Circle City. I think we should build a raft and float to the Tanana River."

"What about rapids?" Dillon asked. "We could come to a hasty death. Slow starvation is better. Maybe we can shoot a sheep or a moose. I say we walk."

"What do you say Mac, Sven?" Lt. Castner asked.

"Rafting sounds good to me," McGregor said. "We've walked for three months."

"Rafting," Sven said. He would not disagree with the lieutenant and McGregor."

"Rafting it is," Lieutenant Castner said. "We will build a raft. Tomorrow we will shoot Kid, take his meat for food, and float on our way."

18

"WAKE up!"

Sven rubbed his eyes and stared at the soldier poking his head into the tent.

"Wake up, Sir." Sven shook Lt. Castner's shoulder. "We have company."

"Huh?" Lt. Castner growled from beneath his blanket, "Who's here?"

"Private Canwell, Sir," the stranger said. "I have orders from Captain Glenn."

Lt. Castner sat upright and stared at Pvt. Canwell. "What orders?"

"Wait until Captain Glenn catches up with you."

"Catches up? Where is he?" Lt. Castner asked.

"Close behind on your trail," Canwell replied. "Get your men up. I have supplies for breakfast. Stephen is starting a fire and we'll eat soon."

Sven pulled on his worn boots and stepped from the tent. The smell of coffee and bacon whet his appetite. He hurried to the fire where Stephen, a native, cooked breakfast.

"Hungry?" Stephen asked.

"We all are," Sven said. "We haven't had much to eat."

"Now eat plenty," Stephen said. "Get plate."

"Stephen is a good cook," Pvt. Canwell said as Stephen

served biscuits and bacon and coffee. "Captain Glenn hired him in Knik."

"Know Billy," Stephen said. "Saw Billy, two men, on trail."

"When?" Lt. Castner asked.

"Hour, two hours."

"This morning," Canwell said. "We passed them about three miles back."

"They stole a tent, food, and other things yesterday," Lt. Castner said. "Mac, get your gun. We'll chase those natives home and retrieve our tent and supplies. Stephen, can you lead us to their camp?"

"I lead," Stephen said.

"May I go along, Sir?" Sven asked.

"No, stay and help Dillon."

"Doing what?"

"Clean up before Captain Glenn comes."

"Are you going to chase Billy away?"

"No, Sven, I won't chase Billy away. If he wants, he may return here," Lt. Castner answered. "He belongs with us."

"Good," Sven said and smiled.

Sven cleaned his and the others' metal plates with sand and rinsed them in the stream, he folded their blankets, and he groomed Kid as he waited for Lt. Castner to return.

"How are you doing, Kid," Sven talked as he worked. "I bet you're glad Captain Glenn is coming. That means Mac doesn't have to shoot you and we won't eat you. What is good for you may be bad for me. I am afraid that Captain Glenn will order us to return to Knik, and I won't get to Circle City to find my father. What do you think, Kid? Do you want ..."

"Sven!"

Sven turned as Billy interrupted his work.

"Billy back."

"Why did you run away?" Sven asked.

"No run. Afraid. Man have knife. Say come." Billy showed how one of the men had threatened him.

"I am happy that you are back," Sven said and gave Billy a half hug.

"Billy happy here." He hugged Sven. "We go?"

"No, we wait for Captain Glenn. He has orders for Lieutenant Castner. That is what Private Canwell and Stephen came to tell him. Do you know Stephen?"

"Billy know. He from Knik."

"Here they come," McGregor called and pointed.

Sven ran to a small rise and stood beside Lt. Castner. They watched the men with five pack mules hike single file toward them. Sven recognized Cpl. Young and Mr. Hicks, and Privates Evans and Dillinger.

Lt. Castner saluted as his commanding officer approached. "Welcome, Captain Glenn. I did not expect to see you here."

"You travel fast," Capt. Glenn replied. "I expected to catch you long before now. I see you still have young Sven with you. Is he the reason you're going so fast?" He smiled at Sven.

Sven grinned and said, "It is good to see you, Sir."

"Sven has been a big help, Sir," Lt. Castner said. "His skill with the mules has helped a great deal."

"We've been on your trail ever since I met Young and Hicks almost a month ago. You know most of these men," Capt. Glenn said, "but there is someone I wish you to meet." He waved for a civilian to join them.

"Lieutenant Castner, this is geologist Walter Mendenhall. He is helping write reports and is expert at making maps. He has a surprise for you."

After shaking hands, Mr. Mendenhall unrolled a map and pointed. "Here's the glacier you crossed a few days ago. I hope you approve."

Sven looked at the map. *Castner Glacier* was written across the glacier. "It's named for you, Sir," he said.

"So it is, Sven," Lt. Castner said and grinned, "and I approve. Thank you, Mr. Mendenhall, and thank you, Captain. May I make a request, Sir?"

"You may," Capt. Glenn replied. "What is it?"

"We camped by this large lake, Sir, with mountain ranges in view in every direction. It was so beautiful that

I named it Lake Adah, for my girlfriend. Could you write that on your map?"

"I think we named that lake already," Capt. Glenn replied. "I could get into trouble if I change it. I wrote my wife about it and sent the letter to Knik to be sent home."

"Look," Mr. Mendenhall said. "I think this is the lake you mean. We named it Lake Louise for Captain Glenn's wife. Do you want it named Lake Adah?"

Lt. Castner shook his head. "I guess not. Perhaps you can name another lake for her."

"Thank you, Lieutenant," Captain Glenn said and placed an arm around Lt. Castner's back. "Now tell me how you have fared. We saw evidence along the trail, remains of the mule and horse, that show you are in trouble."

Sven joined Billy and Mr. Hicks as the two officers talked.

The combined units traveled down what Mr. Mendenhall said was the Delta River. Sven enjoyed the slower pace as he talked with his soldier friends, and those he only knew from Ladd's Station. He ate himself full at every meal.

When he remembered to pray, Sven gave thanks that there was now plenty of food and he had warmer clothes. Best of all, he gave thanks that they did not turn back. In a week or two he would find his father in Circle City.

After a week of downstream travel together, Capt. Glenn addressed the men at breakfast. "Lieutenant Castner and I have been discussing the advance of this expedition. We do not have sufficient supplies for all of us to reach Circle City. Most of you will return to Knik and back to Vancouver Barracks in Washington with me.

"Lieutenant Castner will fulfill our orders by leading a small command to Circle City on the Yukon River. He expects to arrive there in ten days. I want two volunteers to accompany him."

McGregor stood up. "I will go, Sir. I've come this far, and I promised to be responsible for Sven."

"Thank you, McGregor."

"Captain, Sir, Mac is my good friend," said a red-bearded private whose name Sven did not remember, "and I would like to go with him. It will be my first opportunity to be with a lead group, and, if I have to say so, I am the best man for this expedition."

The other soldiers, accustomed to Blitch's bragging, smiled. Sven wondered why any soldier would boast like that. He had been taught to be humble; that he should let what he did show what type of person he was.

"Thank you, Blitch," Capt. Glenn said, "That makes two. Now everyone pack up. We'll go our separate ways today. Sven."

"Yes, Sir."

"You are welcome to return with me," Capt. Glenn said, "and be back home with your mother before winter. If you are determined to continue to Circle City, you may accompany Lieutenant Castner."

Sven looked from the captain to the lieutenant. The thought of being home with his mother tempted him.

Lt. Castner smiled and said, "It's your choice. You may come with me, but even then we do not know if you will find your father."

Sven bit his lip and replied, "I've come this far, Sir. I will find my father and return home with him."

"I thought you would say that," Lt. Castner said. "Get your things."

Sven wrapped his blanket and Mackinaw inside his slicker and stuffed them into his pack with his plate and eating utensils. Everything else he owned he wore.

"Are you ready?" Capt. Glenn asked as Sven stood before him with Lt. Castner and Privates McGregor and Blitch.

"Yes, Sir," they answered together.

"Good. You have those two mules, Weyler and Jack. I had them loaded with twenty days of supplies. Lieutenant, when you arrive at Circle City catch a steamboat to St. Michael and a ship from there back to Washington. And Sven, I hope you find your father and return home safely. God bless you all."

Sven saluted with the others as Capt. Glenn turned away. Sven led the mule Weyler behind Lt. Castner. McGregor and Blitch followed with Jack. The nippy chill of Alaska's early autumn hastened their steps.

———

Late that afternoon they gazed across a broad river.

"That's the Tanana," Lt. Castner said. "Circle City is not far away."

"How do we cross?" Blitch asked.

"We will ford if we can find a shallow place. Follow me," Lt. Castner ordered. He led the way downstream.

"Come on, Weyler," Sven said as he gently tugged the mule's lead rope. "It's not far anymore. Not after we cross this river."

19

"LOOK, a cabin," Sven said and pointed. A small log cabin stood nearly hidden in the trees.

"Let's take a look," Lt. Castner said. "There's no sense walking farther downstream when we must go upstream on the other side. We'll build a raft. Hello. Is anyone here?"

When no one answered, he pushed open the door.

"We'll have a roof over our heads tonight. Mac, Blitch, unload the mules," Lt. Castner ordered. "Sven, put our packs inside and care for the mules."

"Where are you going, Sir?" Blitch asked as Lt. Castner walked away.

The lieutenant did not answer as he looked at trees near the river. With his hatchet he marked three trees.

"Mac, Blitch," Lt. Castner called, "bring axes and the saw. We'll use these trees for our raft."

As the men felled and trimmed the trees, Sven collected branches to use for firewood.

"Sven, get Weyler and Jack and pull these logs to the bank," Lt. Castner ordered. "I'll find something to tie them together."

"Why not use our rope?" McGregor asked.

"I don't want to cut it. We may need it," Lt. Castner said. "Was there anything in the cabin, Sven?"

"An old moose hide. There's no rope."

Sven tied one end of their rope to Jack's harness as Blitch tied the other end to a log.

"Come on, Jack," Sven whispered in the mule's ear and led it toward the river.

After three short trips the logs lay side by side on the bank.

"I hope the owner won't mind," Lt. Castner said when he returned from the cabin. "I cut up his moose hide. Blitch, help me here. Mac and Sven, cook something to eat."

"I'll start a fire," Sven said. He peeled bark from a birch tree and lit a fire as McGregor opened the food packs.

"Dang it all, something's wrong," McGregor said and swore. "This doesn't look like enough to feed us for twenty days."

"Are you sure, Mac?" Sven looked into the pack. "It looks like plenty."

"Well, it's not enough." McGregor cut up meat and potatoes and dropped them into a pot of water. He sprinkled in salt and threw in a few carrots. "Stew tonight. We will have to ration our food."

"We got cheated," McGregor said as the lieutenant and Blitch approached the cabin. "There is not enough food."

"What?" Lt. Castner asked. "There should be enough for twenty days?"

"I don't think so. See for yourself," McGregor said.

Lt. Castner inspected their supplies. "You're right, Mac. Someone fouled up. There's only enough for ten days."

"What will we do?" Blitch asked. "Can we catch up with Captain Glenn?"

"No, we won't turn back. It will take one day to cross the river and two days up the Volkmar River. After that it's downhill to Circle City. In ten days we should be there." Lt. Castner replied. "Eat. Tomorrow we cross the Tanana."

———

"Hello, the camp." The call from midstream surprised them as they prepared to cross the Tanana in the morning.

Two white men steered a raft toward their camp.

"Hello, and welcome," Lt. Castner greeted them as they stepped ashore.

"Headed downstream?" the elder of the prospectors asked.

"No, across the river."

"What for?"

"We are heading up the Volkmar, going to Circle City."

"You won't get there," the younger man said.

"There's no trail," the older man said. "We went fifty miles up the river and there is no place to go."

"Thanks, but we'll try the Volkmar," Lt. Castner said. "My map shows that it is a short river. You must have been on a different river."

"You will find out we were right," the older prospector said. "Let's go, Frank. No sense wasting time with fools."

The two men poled their raft into the current and floated downstream.

"It is time for us to go too," Lt. Castner said.

"What if they are right?" Blitch asked. "Let's stay in the cabin until the rain stops. Then we should follow them."

Sven wondered why Blitch had volunteered to accompany Lt. Castner. If Blitch had his way they might never get to Circle City.

"I'm in command here," Lt. Castner said. "We're going up the Volkmar, rain or shine. Blitch, you're going on the first crossing."

"Yes, Sir," Blitch responded, "but I think I am right."

Lt. Castner ignored Blitch's remark, but McGregor laughed and said, "You always think you are right."

"Sven, get Weyler. The mule will have to swim behind us." Lt. Castner ordered.

"Yes, Sir."

Sven tied a blindfold over Weyler's eyes and led him to the water. "Come on, Weyler. You can make it." He tugged gently on the lead rope as Lt. Castner and Blitch poled the raft into the cold Tanana River.

After they crossed the river, Sven led the way as they towed the raft upstream. Using his hatchet, Sven chopped shrubs away from the shoreline so Weyler could pull the raft.

"Far enough," Lt. Castner said after an hour. "I should be able to get back to Mac from here. You two keep chopping a trail toward the Volkmar."

"Yes, Sir. Where's the axe?" Blitch asked.

"On the raft."

"It's not here, Sir. No axe, no hatchet. They must have slipped through the cracks," Blitch said.

"Do what you can. Sven has a hatchet. Blaze trees so we can follow. There's enough food for two meals, tonight's and tomorrow's breakfast. If Mac and I don't make it today, we should catch you by noon tomorrow. I'll go back."

Sven watched as Lt. Castner poled the unruly raft back across the river. Blitch sat with his back against a tree and closed his eyes.

"Shouldn't we be going, Sir?" Sven asked Blitch.

"I'm resting, and don't call me sir. I'm not a no-good officer. Call me Blitch like everyone does."

"Yes, Sir ... Blitch," Sven answered and wondered why Blitch sounded so mean. He wished he were with McGregor or Lt. Castner.

"How are you doing, Weyler," Sven whispered in the mule's ear as he hobbled it. "Why, you're shivering. That cold swim chilled you, didn't it?" He rubbed Weyler's back and sides with the sleeves of his Mackinaw.

"Wait here." He stroked the mule's nose. "I'm going to start blazing a trail."

Slash, slash. Sven marked both sides of a tree and looked at Blitch. The soldier did not look up. Sven hacked brush and cut a narrow path along the river bank. Every ten steps he slashed a tree on both sides. He would follow Lt. Castner's orders even if Blitch would not.

Sven turned back at a small grassy clearing. He found Blitch sitting against the same tree, but awake and eating a raw potato.

"Blitch, I found a place to camp tonight."

"Good," Blitch growled. "Load the mule."

Sven unhobbled Weyler. "I need your help."

"What good are you?" Blitch asked. He slowly stood up and helped lift the heavy tents and other supplies onto Weyler's back.

Sven led Weyler and started following the trail he had cut.

"Who made you leader?" Blitch asked. "I'm not following any baby-faced boy. I'll go first."

"Yes, Blitch."

"Which way?"

Sven stared at Blitch and wondered how one man could be so lazy, so mean, and so stupid. "Follow the cut shrubs and blaze marks on the trees."

At the clearing Sven unloaded Weyler, and unrolled a tent.

"What are you doing?" Blitch asked.

"I thought we would camp here tonight."

"You did, did you, Babyface? I'm in charge. We camp where I say."

Sven bit his lip and ignored Blitch's name calling. "I know, Blitch. We will go on if you say. Here, take the hatchet."

Blitch looked at the hatchet and shook his head. "We'll camp here. Set up the tent, then make a fire and cook our meal. I will shoot a rabbit."

Blitch took his rifle and walked into the woods.

Sven watched him go and set to work. Meat and potatoes sizzled in the frying pan before Blitch returned.

"I didn't see any rabbits," Blitch said.

Sven wondered if he had looked. He had returned exactly when the food was ready to eat.

Sven prayed for Lt. Castner and McGregor to join them so he would not be alone with Blitch, but the two did not come that evening.

The next morning Blitch ordered, "Start a fire, Babyface, and call me when the coffee is ready."

Sven pulled on his shoes and stepped from the tent. A moose stood near Weyler. He watched it as he lit a fire and set the coffee pot in the coals. He mixed batter for hotcakes.

"Coffee ready yet?" Blitch called from the tent.

"Not yet," Sven shouted. He did not want Blitch to shoot the moose. He knew Blitch would make him skin and butcher it. "I'll call you."

Sven smiled when his shout had its desired affect. The moose pricked up his ears, looked at Sven, and trotted away among the trees.

Sven waited a few minutes before calling Blitch.

"We will stay here until Mac and the lieutenant come," Blitch said as they ate. "They should be here by noon."

"Shouldn't we blaze more trail?" Sven asked. "That's what Lieutenant Castner said for us to do."

"He's not here, so I am in charge. We will wait. I don't intend to do all the work."

"I will blaze more trail if it's all right with you." Sven remained determined to get to Circle City and wondered if Blitch would do any work to help him get there.

"Do what you want," Blitch said. "I'm staying here."

Part Three

DESPERATION

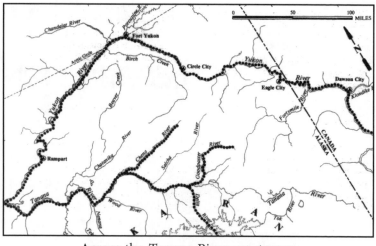

Across the Tanana River, upstream,
and back downstream on the Volkmar River
(since renamed the Goodpastor River),
by water on the Tanana River, with a sidetrip
up the Chena River, to the Yukon River,
and by dogsled from Rampart into Canada,
September, 1898, to January, 1899.

20

SVEN blazed a narrow trail along the Tanana River. To scare animals away he sang songs his mother had taught him. Thinking of his mother saddened him. He realized that he should not have run away, but he thought how happy she would be when he returned to Minnesota with his father. What he thought would take a few weeks had already taken almost five months. He swung his hatchet faster and sang louder. Circle City was now a week away.

He worked until he saw fish swimming up a small stream. His mouth watered as the thought of eating salmon.

After trimming alder saplings into stakes, he waded into the stream and pushed them into the river bottom. He sharpened one sapling into a spear as Billy had done.

He collected wood and lit a fire for baking and smoking fish. As he worked he watched for fish to swim into his funnel. None came.

He cut more stakes and placed them closer together and farther across the stream, but no fish came.

Tired of waiting, Sven pulled his pan from his pack and scooped up some gravel. If I can't catch fish, he thought, perhaps I can find gold.

As he panned, he moved upstream. At a bend in the stream, one pan of gravel held several flecks of gold. He scooped deeper. The second pan held two small nuggets.

Sven scooped again. Another nugget. He scooped gravel and swished it around in his pan again and again. He found many small nuggets, the size of shotgun shot, which he slipped into his leather pouch beneath his shirt.

Sven forgot about fishing until a salmon splashed in the middle of the stream. He hurried to his funnel trap. Three salmon swam in circles near the shore. Sven tried to spear them. He succeeded after driving each fish so close to shore and his stakes that he could not miss.

He placed four chunks of one fish on rocks in the coals. The other fish he cut into strips and hung in the smoke. He would have fish for Lt. Castner, McGregor, and Blitch when they caught up with him.

He wondered where they were. Lt. Castner had said that McGregor and he would arrive before noon. Clouds hid the sun but Sven's hunger told him it was past noon. He speared two more fish and hung the meat over the fire to smoke. He ate one piece of roast salmon and wrapped the other pieces in leaves. He would bring roast fish to the others on the trail.

———

"Where have you been, Babyface?" Blitch growled when Sven walked back into their camp.

"Cutting trail and fishing," Sven said. "I brought fish to add to our meal."

"What meal. We don't have any food."

"We will when Lieutenant Castner and Mac get here," Sven said.

"Haven't you noticed," Blitch said, "it's getting dark. Something happened to them. They're not coming so let me have the fish."

"I only have two pieces," Sven lied. "I was going to cut them in half." He took two of the wrapped pieces from his pack.

"I'll eat one. You eat one," Blitch said. "It is all we

132

have." Blitch snatched one piece and ate greedily. "Do you have anymore?"

"No." Sven decided to save the other roast piece and the smoked strips until morning.

He walked toward Weyler. "What is the matter, old mule? Why are you lying here? Get up." He unhobbled the mule's legs and tugged at its lead rope until it stood. "You need some exercise. Are you sick?"

The mule's head drooped and it stumbled along as Sven led it in a circle around the clearing. "Did you eat today? Are you lonely? Do you miss Jack?"

"There's nothing wrong with it," Blitch said and laughed. "It's a mule. Quit talking to it. We need to get some sleep. If the lieutenant and Mac don't get here early tomorrow we'll build a raft and float downstream after the prospectors we saw yesterday."

Sven hobbled Weyler and joined Blitch in the tent. As he lay down he prayed that Lt. Castner and McGregor would come. He dreaded the thought of another day alone with Blitch.

———

"Start a fire, Babyface," Blitch said the next morning, and prodded Sven with his foot. "Boil water for coffee."

Sven crawled from the tent and lit a fire. He ate his roast fish before Blitch came from the tent.

Weyler lay on the ground again. Sven unhobbled it and tugged it to its feet. "I wish I could make you feel better."

"Leave that mule alone," Blitch said as he drank weak coffee made from yesterday's grounds. "Do you have anymore fish?"

"A couple of strips of smoked salmon." Sven handed Blitch two small pieces. "I left some where I caught the fish."

"Babyface, you are as stupid as that mule."

"Quit calling me Babyface," Sven answered angrily. "I didn't expect to return here. I thought you were smart enough to follow me there."

"You thought wrong. Now chop down that tree," Blitch said and pointed toward a tall pine. "We'll build a raft."

Sven chopped as Blitch sat and watched.

"How could you be so stupid?" Blitch asked as the tree fell into the river. "How will you trim the branches off now?"

Sven chopped through the remaining part of the trunk as the tree swung into shore and grounded into the gravel.

He handed Blitch the hatchet. "It seemed like the best way to get the log into the water," he said. "It will float after you chop off the branches."

He picked up his pack and walked over to the mule and whispered in its ear. "Come on, Weyler. You and I are going to Circle City. I saw Lieutenant Castner's map and we will find our way. I'm not going to float on a raft with that lazy man." He led Weyler to the trail he had made.

"Where do you think you are going, Babyface?" Blitch yelled.

"To check my smoked salmon."

"Leave the mule."

"Weyler needs the exercise." Sven walked away, leaving Blitch and his swearing behind.

Sven stared at bear tracks on the river bank and around the ashes of his fire. Seeing four fish swimming in his trap, he rekindled his fire. He needed food to hike to Circle City. He sang loudly and prayed that the bear would not return.

———

One fish roasted in the fire and strips of the other three smoked over the flames when Lt. Castner, McGregor, and Blitch found him.

"It looks like you've been busy, Sven," Lt. Castner greeted him.

"Yes, Sir. The fish should be ready soon."

"Blitch said you deserted him this morning when he

thought Mac and I weren't coming. You took the mule and ran away when he wanted to build a raft."

Sven looked at Blitch who scowled at him and curled his fist.

Sven bit his lip. "Yes, Sir. I thought the fastest way to get to Circle City would be the way you showed me on the map. It would be the quickest way to find my father."

Lt. Castner draped his arm over Sven's shoulders. "I'm sure it will be the fastest, but it wasn't the smartest. You would have had trouble by yourself. Look at these bear tracks. You need to stay with Blitch or Mac or me or you won't get to Circle City."

"Yes, Sir. Why didn't you and Mac come yesterday?"

"We couldn't force Jack to enter the water. We should have had you with us. Mac remembered this morning that we should blindfold Jack. He swam behind us with a blindfold on."

"Did you dry him and give him a rubdown?" Sven asked. "Weyler is sick and I think it is because of his cold swim."

"We will eat and then you may look after the mules. But we do need to hurry," Lt. Castner said. "Our food supply won't last long and we lost a day of travel yesterday."

—— ——

Both mules, after being chilled in the Tanana River, were sickly. When Sven fell behind with Weyler, Lt. Castner said, "That mule is slowing us down and we need to make better time. The mule will have to fend for itself."

Sven held back tears as he helped unload the pack from Weyler. He rubbed its nose and whispered "Good-bye" as they left it on the river bank.

The men and Sven also weakened. The strain of cutting a trail sapped their strength and they abandoned the heavy tents that Weyler had carried. A light, steady drizzle soaked them. That evening Lt. Castner ordered them to begin eating half rations.

"What day is it?" Sven asked as they ate a skimpy meal of beans and smoked salmon.

"September four," Lt. Castner replied.

Sven sighed and a tear rolled down each cheek.

"So, Sven, what's the matter?" McGregor asked when he saw the tears. "Is the trip getting to be too much for you?"

"It's not that, Mac." Sven wiped the tears onto his sleeve. "It's my fifteenth birthday. I was thinking of my mother. She always makes something special for birthdays. It's the first time I won't be home for my birthday."

"Happy birthday," McGregor said and patted Sven's shoulder. "Cheer up; in a week you can celebrate with your father."

Will I, Sven wondered as he curled himself up under his torn slicker. Under the low branches of a spruce tree, he lay on the wet ground with the men and tried to sleep.

21

"THIS should be the Volkmar River," Lt. Castner said as he stepped into the water the following afternoon. "If that is an island, we are at the mouth of the Volkmar."

Sven, McGregor, and Blitch waded behind him without concern for their footwear. They were wet from the continuing drizzle. Safely across, they followed Lt. Castner on a trail the led along the shoreline.

"Here's a cabin," Lt. Castner said in surprise as he entered a clearing. "Somebody must live here. Hello."

When no one answered he pushed the door open, ducked his head and entered. The others crowded in behind him. Dried fish and jerky hung from the ceiling and baskets of berries sat on a shelf.

Blitch grabbed a handful of berries and popped some into his mouth.

"Leave them, Blitch," Lt. Castner ordered.

"What? We need food. I'm starving."

"No," Lt. Castner said, "the owners might return and need it worse than we do."

"Nobody needs it worse than we do," Blitch argued.

"Get out of the cabin," Lt. Castner ordered. "Let's be sure we are on an island and have found the Volkmar. In a few days we will be in Circle City."

"Are you sure we can make it?" McGregor asked. "What about what those prospectors said?"

"They were wrong," Lt. Castner said. "We don't have far to go and we won't waste time here."

Sven sighed in relief. He hated Blitch's complaints and McGregor's questions. Lt. Castner had maps and would lead them to Circle City. He stepped out into the drizzle. As he glanced back he saw Blitch snatch pieces of jerky and stuff them into his pocket.

———

Lt. Castner led them up the Volkmar River. They progressed slowly. Each step became a struggle as they waded through swamps, climbed hills, forded streams, battled brush, and tramped over rough rocks. Rotting footwear offered little support or comfort for their sore feet.

Sven, following Lt. Castner's example, tried to be cheerful. Often he felt like complaining the way Blitch did, and thought it would have been wise to take food from the cabin. Their supply dwindled rapidly. Sven knew he was losing strength as each step became more difficult.

He trailed behind as they hiked along the river bank when he heard McGregor yell, "Lieutenant! Sven, help Lieutenant Castner!"

Lt. Castner, bobbing along in the swift current, struggled to keep his head above the surface. McGregor and Blitch scrambled along the bank, trying to catch him. Sven gasped at the sight and raced after the lieutenant.

"Ahhh!" Lt. Castner cried as he crashed into a log jam. He clutched his sketching case with maps, reports and diary as he climbed from the chilling water.

"Are you all right, Sir?" Sven asked,

"I think so. I lost our last axe but saved my papers. Build a fire. I need to warm up."

Sven collected wood as McGregor lit a fire.

"Doesn't that convince you, Lieutenant? We should go back before we die out here," Blitch said as they huddled around the fire. "If I were in charge we would raft down the Tanana River."

"You are not in charge, so quit complaining," Lt. Castner replied. "We have orders to obey, and Circle City isn't far."

As soon as he had warmed himself, the lieutenant led the way upstream. With each mile they walked, their misery increased. Their clothes, shredded into rags, decorated the brush. Their foot coverings wore out and they walked barefoot on the cold, wet ground.

"Stupid mule," McGregor said and swore when Jack stumbled and fell into the river.

Sven knelt in the river and whispered in the mule's ear. "Come on, Jack, get up. We need you."

The mule rose and stepped out of the water. Sven coaxed, but it stood shivering and refused to take another step.

"Shoot him," Lt. Castner ordered. "We don't have time to waste."

Sven turned his back and held his hands over his ears as McGregor pulled the trigger. They butchered the mule and took as much meat as they could carry.

They plodded on. Rain and wet snow made walking difficult. In their weak conditions their pace slowed. To speed up they discarded gear as they hiked. Extra compasses, a barometer, cooking utensils, even their blankets were abandoned.

Each day Blitch complained. "Let's turn back. There's food in that cabin. I'm starving."

September fifteenth, ten days after leaving the cabin, Lt. Castner ordered, "Today we will climb to higher ground."

"And then what?" Blitch asked.

"If we see a pass through the mountains we'll go for it. If not we'll return to the Tanana River."

As they climbed from the valley, Sven muttered a prayer, asking that they would see a pass.

"What are you mumbling about?" Blitch asked and laughed. "Lieutenant, Sven is going crazy; he's talking to himself."

"I'm praying," Sven said. "I haven't been praying every day like I should."

"Praying?" Blitch laughed. "Now I know you're crazy. Why did you keep this baby-faced boy along, Lieutenant? He's crazy."

"Leave him alone, Blitch," McGregor said. "He has been a great help, and we can use all the help we can get."

Lt. Castner had climbed ahead, but from atop a high ridge he saw no pass through the mountains.

"I'm sorry, Men," Lieutenant Castner said as they stood dejectedly together. "The Volkmar must be much longer than my map shows. We have come almost one hundred miles. Tomorrow we will return to the Tanana River. Camp here."

"If we don't die first," Blitch said. "You should have listened to me."

Sven and McGregor built a fire and they ate the last mule meat. Cold air chilled them and snow fell as they huddled around the fire and tried to sleep. Sven's threadbare Mackinaw did little to keep him warm and his torn slicker did not keep him dry. He bit his lip and blinked back tears as he thought about dying without seeing his mother again.

"Let's go, Men," Lt. Castner ordered the next morning. He led them back to the Volkmar and down stream toward the Tanana.

That evening McGregor caught the smallest of rodents, a pica. It provided less than a mouthful for each man. They slept under a spruce tree.

The following morning standing water was frozen and

snow covered the crusted ground. They killed two small ducks for food. On the third day of the retreat downstream, breakfast was boiled roots and root coffee. During the day they nibbled on berries and rose hips and roots and stayed warm by moving.

Late that afternoon McGregor spotted a wolf with three pups.

"Quiet," Lt. Castner whispered. "Mac, you're our best shot. Be ready."

As one curious pup approached nearer and nearer Sven hoped it would return to its mother. He turned his head as McGregor slowly raised the rifle.

Bang!

"Great shot!" Lt. Castner yelled. "Fresh meat tonight."

Sven watched as McGregor skinned and gutted the young wolf.

That evening they camped where they had abandoned their blankets and dined on wolf meat. They ate the nourishing heart, liver, and kidneys first.

That night they curled up around the fire with full stomachs and their blankets wrapped around them.

Three days later they were completely out of food. As they halted at noon, Lt. Castner said, "I have an idea. We'll build a raft and go faster."

"How?" Blitch asked. "We don't have an ax."

"Fire."

They built their raft from fallen spruce trees, burning the logs to equal lengths and hacking off branches with their knives. They tore their blankets into strips to tie the logs together.

"Let's be on our way," Lt. Castner ordered the next morning. Sven sat behind McGregor on the narrow raft, with

Blitch and Lt. Castner behind him. McGregor and Lieutenant Castner held long poles to guide them.

"Here we go." Lt. Castner shoved them into the current.

———

Cold water splashed over them as they raced downstream through foaming white water. Sven ducked behind McGregor and held on as the raft bucked and plunged, pounded through rapids, collided with logs, and scraped under low hanging trees.

"We're going to crash!" McGregor yelled. He vaulted forward as the raft rammed a log jam.

Sven, Blitch, and Lt. Castner pitched into the water.

McGregor, who could not swim, scrambled to shore over the logs. Sven climbed up on the logs and followed him. Lt. Castner and Blitch tried to retrieve their belongings as the raft pounded under the logs. Guns, blankets, cooking utensils, everything was lost.

"We sure were stupid. Lost everything. Rafting was a bad idea," Blitch complained as they stood shivering.

"I'm sorry," Lt. Castner said, "but we didn't lose everything. I saved my map, and my matches are dry. Get some wood."

"And I saved my cup." Blitch held up his cup and laughed bitterly. "Lieutenant's map and matches and my cup will keep us from starving. Ha. We're going to die here."

Lt. Castner ignored Blitch. He took a match from its waterproof container and, using birch bark and the wood Sven and McGregor gathered, started a fire.

Blitch's words echoed in Sven's ears as he warmed and dried himself. "How far is it to the cabin?" he asked. "I don't want to die here."

22

"NONE of us want to die here, Sven," Lt. Castner said. "Let's go, Men."

From the disaster site they trudged ten miles to the bones of the mule Jack. Using canvas and straps they had left, they fashioned shoes and coverings for themselves.

Each of the next five days as they hiked toward the Tanana River, Sven wondered if they would survive. He thought about his mother and how foolish he had been to run away. He could be with her in Minnesota now. He thought about his father and became angry at him for leaving his mother alone with the family. He wouldn't be starving and freezing if it weren't for his father. He prayed and, to keep his sanity, he softly sang songs his mother had taught him.

Lt. Castner walked ahead and said little except, "Don't give up, Men. We will make it."

McGregor trudged beside Sven. He continuously mumbled, telling Sven his life story, how he had run away from home to join the army, to fight, he said, not to starve and freeze in Alaska. McGregor's hopeless words discouraged Sven, so he sang louder.

Blitch plodded along behind them. "Quit singing,"

he yelled at Sven. "We are going to die. What is there to sing about?"

———

The four survived by plucking cranberries and rose hips each time they found them. When they camped at night they drank hot river water, boiled in Blitch's tin cup.   T h e y stopped early each afternoon and gathered enough wood to keep from freezing. At night they crowded close to the fire.

Each morning Sven wondered if he or any of them would live another day. As he looked at the men he wondered how he looked. Their faces were dirty and sallow; light had faded from their eyes. Their tattered clothes draped loosely over meatless skin and bones.

They and he, almost barefooted, shuffled along, and cuts on their feet became festering sores, full of dirt and yellow pus. Each of them stopped often to scrape snow from between his toes. In the mornings, to ease their pain while walking, they broke the crust from the sores. Blood stains on the snow marked their progress as they hobbled forward.

Sven knew he must look as emaciated, as much skin and bones as the others, and he winced with each step he took.

Blitch's complaints accented their desperation. "How much farther, Lieutenant? It will be your fault if we die. I'm hungry. I can't wait to get to the food we saw."

"Quit complaining," McGregor usually answered. "Don't remind me how hungry I am. We'll get there."

Sven wondered if McGregor believed what he said.

When he could push thoughts of death from his mind, Sven prayed and hoped that they would find the food they saw in the cabin. If they reached that cabin they would be saved.

———

Twenty days after they started upstream, they returned to the mouth of the Volkmar River.

"There's the island," Lt. Castner said and pointed across the broad shallow river mouth. "Food."

"At last," McGregor said and shuffled into the cold water. Sven, Lt. Castner, and Blitch waded after him.

"Listen!" McGregor stopped in midstream and held up his hand. "Someone's chopping wood."

No doubt about it! All heard the distinct *Thunk, Thunk, Thunk.*

"People," Lt. Castner declared. "Come on." He led as they splashed toward the island.

Emaciated, dirty, wild looking, they crashed through the brush as quickly as their weary legs would carry them. Their noisy approach attracted a native woman who was repairing a canoe. She took one look, screamed and fled.

"Wait," Lt. Castner called, and tried to follow her.

Five native men armed with rifles stopped them. Lt. Castner raised his hand, palm forward. The natives stared at them.

After a long look one man stepped forward and asked in English, "White man plenty hungry?"

"Plenty hungry," Lt. Castner replied. "White man not eat for six sleeps."

"Come. Plenty moose, plenty caribou, plenty fish. White man eat." They followed the natives to the log cabin.

Sven sank wearily down upon a caribou pelt a native placed on the floor. Tears of joy trickled down his cheek as he watched native women prepare food for them. Hope replaced despair; he would find his father and return to his mother.

A native woman smiled as she gestured for Sven to eat and handed him a bowl of salmon-egg soup. He gulped it down.

He greedily gobbled down the second course of boiled salmon.

"Don't eat too fast," Lt. Castner warned, but he ate as fast as the others did, and washed his salmon down with tea.

"We are going to be sick. Our stomachs won't accept

all this food," Lt. Castner said when the women brought them roast caribou.

"Who cares?" Blitch said. "It's food."

Sven smiled. It was the first time he heard Blitch sound happy, and he felt as Blitch did. He ate as much as his stomach would hold.

Two hours later the women served them a second similar meal. In the middle of the night they ate a third full meal.

"I can't believe it," Lt. Castner said several times. "We should be sick."

"Must be the tea," McGregor said. "My mother always said that tea was good for the stomach."

So did my mother, Sven thought as he stretched out on the caribou hide. "Thank you," he mumbled as a woman covered him with a large bear fur.

———

Sven was alone in the cabin when he awoke. He stretched and stood up. On sore feet he hobbled to the door.

Lt. Castner, McGregor, and Blitch, dressed in moose skin trousers and jackets, sat on a log and leaned against the cabin. A native man and two women rubbed bear grease on the men's sore feet.

"This help," the English speaking native said. "Feel good."

As Sven stepped from the door the two women grabbed him by the arms and pulled him toward the river. He squirmed but could not get away as they tore his ragged clothes off him. He swatted their hands away from the leather pouch as they tried to tear it from around his neck. They pushed him into the cold water and one of them pantomimed scrubbing.

As quickly as he could, Sven rubbed his hands over his body and splashed water over his head. Cold but refreshed, and trying to hide his nakedness, he scrambled from the water. The women, laughing at his embarrassment, dried him with a blanket and helped him into warm moose skin clothing. They led him back to the cabin where the man applied bear grease to his feet.

"Good sleep?" the man asked.

"Yes."

"Good bath?" the man asked and laughed.

"Yes, thank you," Sven answered and smiled. How long had it been since he felt so clean and warm?

"What is so precious in that pouch you are hiding?" Blitch asked.

Sven did not answer.

"Did you hear me, Sven? Lieutenant make him tell."

Sven shook his head as he looked at Lt. Castner.

"He doesn't have to tell you," Lt. Castner said. "You don't have to know."

"Yes, I do," Blitch argued and leered at Sven. "That looks like my pouch that disappeared after we crossed the river. He must have stolen it the day we were alone. That's why he took the mule and ran away."

"That's a lie," Sven said angrily and pulled the pouch from beneath his shirt. "Look, Sir. It is the pouch you had Mac give to me. It has my gold in it."

"Gold?" all three soldiers asked in surprise.

Sven bit his lip. In his anger he had disclosed his secret.

He saw Lt. Castner and McGregor smile.

Blitch sneered. "See, Lieutenant, he stole my gold."

Lt. Castner looked at the pouch and said, "You are a liar, Blitch. This is the pouch I had Mac give to Sven. I don't want to hear any more about it."

As Blitch scowled at him, Sven walked away. He sat in the sunlight, leaned against a tree and watched the natives.

The five men, five women, and six children fished for salmon in the Tanana River. The men dip-netted from a small pier. When a salmon was caught, the man tossed it to the bank where one of the children clubbed it. Other children chased birds away from the strips of meat hanging to dry on a wooden frame.

Sven and the men rested and ate and regained their strength. That evening the natives gave them caribou skins to use for bedding. When they chose to sleep under the branches of a tall spruce tree, Sven snuggled himself between Lt. Castner and McGregor. He feared that Blitch might try to steal his gold.

23

"How do you feel?" Lt Castner asked the others in the morning. "I think that we should leave as soon as possible."

"Let's go," McGregor said. "I feel well enough. We don't want to stay here all winter."

"I am ready," Blitch said.

Sven nodded his agreement. Having a full stomach and being warm lifted his spirit. He remained determined to reach Circle City.

"We must go," Lt. Castner said to the English speaking native. "We need canoes."

"No go. Stay here. Cold, snow come."

"No," Lt. Castner said. "We must go. Will you help?"

"I ask," the native said and talked to the other men.

After the natives argued among themselves, three of them agreed to canoe Lt. Castner and his men downstream.

"You go," the native said and pointed to the three. "They take. Two sleeps."

"Good, thank you," Lt. Castner said.

After breakfast they began their trip down the Tanana River. Sven and McGregor canoed with one native; Lt. Castner and Blitch, each with another native.

"It won't be long now," Lt. Castner said as they paddled from shore. "We'll soon be on the Yukon River."

"You said that before," Blitch said. "If we had gone this way a month ago, we'd be there already."

Lt. Castner did not answer.

Sven wondered how long the canoe trip would take. He sat back to back with McGregor in the bottom of the canoe as it floated with the swift current. The native men paddled only to steer and when pulling ashore on a gravel bar or island.

At each stop Lt. Castner asked, "Why are we stopping?"

The natives smiled and gestured but did not answer. During each stop they appeared frightened as they searched the ground, and pointed at each track they saw.

"What do you think they are looking for?" Sven asked.

"Who knows," Lt. Castner replied. "I wish we would keep going."

"It don't do any good to complain, Sir," McGregor said. "They don't know what you are saying, and they wouldn't obey you if they did."

"And we aren't walking," Blitch said, "so don't complain."

Sven smiled at the irony of their main complainer telling someone else not to complain, but he agreed. He enjoyed the canoe ride and the scenery along the river. Complaining would not make them go faster.

In addition to frequent short stops, they stopped five times to eat. That night they built a fire, burning a ten-foot log. The natives lay on one side of the log with their feet toward the fire. Sven, wrapped in his caribou skin blanket, lay between Lt. Castner and McGregor on the other side of the log.

He lay on his back and gazed up into the sky. He recognized the big dipper, high over head and the polar star, and thought of home. His father had pointed out these stars to his sister and him on their farm in Minnesota. He wished they had never left there to move to Seattle. He wished he had never run away to find his father. He could be back in Minnesota now, sleeping in a warm bed.

McGregor shook him awake the next morning. "Breakfast, Sven, and hurry. The natives are ready to go."

Sven finished drinking his root coffee as they canoed downstream.

That evening, after many stops, they landed at a large native camp near the mouth of the Salcha River. Twelve families lived there in birch bark shelters.

Sven, Lt. Castner, McGregor, and Blitch waited as their three native companions talked with the men. They listened and watched the gestures made in their direction.

One man walked toward them. "You stay?" he asked.

"No." Lt. Castner pointed downstream. "We must go."

"Eat. Sleep. Go in morning. Come."

"Good," Lt. Castner agreed.

They followed the man into his birchbark house. Two families shared the shelter, with one family living on each side of the center ridge pole and cooking fire.

The arrival of four white guests excited the women. As they bustled about preparing the meal, one woman's dress caught on fire.

"Yeow!" she screamed and ran about frantically.

Lt. Castner jumped up and tackled her. Sven helped him beat out the flames.

After she had calmed herself, the woman served a meal of tasty stew. As they ate, her husband thanked Lt. Castner and said, "Big smoke canoe. Much white man. Chena River."

"A steamboat?" Lt. Castner asked. "White men?"

Through questioning and the native's gestures they learned that a steamboat had come up the Tanana River and turned up the Chena River. The white men remained there.

"Lieutenant," Blitch said, "if we had rafted down the Tanana right away, we would have met them. You should have listened to me."

"So, Blitch, do you always know what's right? Quit

complaining," McGregor said. "The lieutenant did what he thought was right. He couldn't help it if his maps were wrong."

"Yeah, quit complaining." Sven echoed McGregor's words and immediately wished he hadn't.

Blitch turned on him. "Who asked you anything, Babyface? You shouldn't even be here, eating our food and slowing us down. We should have left you a long time ago."

"Blitch, keep quiet, and don't call Sven Babyface," Lt. Castner ordered. "Sven did his share of the work and did not slow us down."

Sven didn't say another word. Near the wall of the shelter he curled up in his caribou blanket and slept.

———

In the morning they floated downstream, each in a canoe with a man from the Salcha River camp. When the natives saw a bull moose swimming across the river they raced it toward shore. They killed the moose as it climbed from the water. The delay to butcher it added meat to their supplies.

Splitting wood of their birch bark canoes caused long delays each morning. Freezing nights cracked the bark. In the morning the natives heated pine wood to get sap to seal the cracks. But the canoes leaked.

Sven knelt in icy water and bailed with his wooden cup. He listened as Blitch muttered complaints but, like Lt. Castner and McGregor, Sven said nothing. The native he canoed with did not speak English and he did not speak Athabascan.

Sven felt relief when, at the mouth of the Chena River, they arrived at the camp of six native Tanana families. They would soon reach the steamboat.

His hope for reaching the steamboat vanished when Lt. Castner ordered him to stay at the camp with McGregor and Blitch.

"You wait here while I try to get a boat and supplies,"

Lt. Castner ordered. "Wait ten days. If I am not back by then you are free to leave, to find your way to a fort on the Yukon River."

"Yes, Sir," Blitch and McGregor said.

"Hurry back," McGregor added.

Sven watched as Lt. Castner, accompanied by seven natives, canoed up the Chena River. He did not mind being left with his friend McGregor, but he hated being with Blitch. Though his mother had taught him to look for good in everyone, he found nothing likable in Blitch. He did not trust Blitch and wondered why Blitch disliked him.

———

Every morning while they waited for Lt. Castner's return, Blitch nagged Sven. "Sven, cook breakfast. Sven, fetch water. Sven, chop wood for the fire. Sven, let me see your gold." If McGregor wasn't close, he called Sven "Babyface."

Sven bit his lip and worked without answering. He secured the pouch more tightly around his neck, so Blitch could not slip the cord off over his head and steal his gold.

McGregor helped with the camp chores and said to Blitch, "Leave Sven alone. He is doing his share of the work. Why don't you get off your lazy rear end and do something yourself?"

"I like being boss," Blitch said and laughed. "What good is Babyface if we don't let him work for us?"

After breakfast each morning, Sven, sometimes with McGregor, sometimes alone, hiked away from camp. Blitch was too lazy to join them. Together Sven and McGregor fished and caught trout to eat. When he was alone Sven panned for gold but found nothing.

In the evenings Sven and McGregor visited with the friendly natives. They sat in their homes and shared their meal.

Blitch stayed by their own campfire and ate fish. "I

don't like Indians," he said. "They're dirty and have fleas. I've been scratching ever since we left the Salcha River."

"Take a bath," McGregor answered.

———

Each evening Blitch would announce the number of days before they could leave. "Only five days and we can leave. We will be on our own without the lieutenant ordering us around."

"Don't count of it," McGregor answered. "Lieutenant Castner will be back on time."

Sven hoped McGregor was right. He would hate traveling with Blitch without the lieutenant.

At midday of day six some of the native men returned.

"Where is Lieutenant Castner?" McGregor asked the man who understood English.

"He come in slow white man canoe."

"The steamboat?" Sven asked.

"No, little boat. So little, no food."

"No food?" Blitch asked. "No hotcakes for breakfast? We still might starve to death."

———

"Didn't you get any food?" McGregor asked as he, Blitch, and Sven crowded around when Lt. Castner arrived that evening.

"The natives said you got no food," Blitch said.

"They don't know," Lt. Castner whispered. "It's hidden."

"Why?" Blitch asked. "I would like hotcakes for breakfast."

"We won't have them tomorrow. Our friends," Lt. Castner said and nodded toward the natives, "are no longer friendly."

24

"WHY not?" Sven asked as he looked at the natives. They were scowling and talking angrily together.

"They received no food." Lt. Castner answered.

"But you did?" McGregor asked.

"Yes, but the miners there, from your state of Minnesota, Sven, did not want to help. I persuaded them to give me this rowboat. The food is hidden in the air tanks at each end of the boat. I also received two pans so we can cook, and this rifle and some ammunition, and salve for our sore feet. Now get some sleep. We'll leave before breakfast."

"We are leaving," Lt. Castner told the natives the next morning. "Thank you for your help."

As they rowed away, Sven frowned. The natives did not respond to his farewell wave. Natives had saved their lives and been their friends, but now they stood, rifles in hand, watching. A few, waving rifles and shouting angrily, followed along the bank.

For five days, from early morning until sundown they floated with the current. Sven sat in the stern, thinking about the strange turns his trip had taken, the good and bad. If ... what great meaning for such a small word. Six months after running away from home he had not found his father. He floated down the Tanana River with three soldiers who hoped to reach the Yukon River, but far away from Circle City.

Each man seemed lost in his own thoughts, and Sven appreciated the silence. Lt. Castner studied his map, the same map that had led him to believe the Volkmar River was only twenty miles long. The map now seemed accurate; streams flowed into the Tanana River according to his map.

"There," the lieutenant said and pointed to his map at each stream passed.

Sven waved to natives who lived in small camps where the streams entered the river.

"Ha," Blitch scoffed. "Do you really believe your map is accurate now?"

Then silence.

How far we have come, Sven thought. Far to the south, through breaks in the scraggly spruce trees that lined the river, he saw the high mountains of the Alaska Range. He saw Denali, the High One, the same majestic mountain he first had seen from Cook Inlet.

Each evening as light faded they camped in a spruce grove. They ate well. The miners from the Chena River had given them plenty of food. As each night seemed colder than the previous night, they huddled closer to the fire.

"We will take turns keeping the fire going," Lt. Castner ordered. "We don't want to burn our clothes again, so one of us must stay awake. Sven, take the first two hours; then Mac; then Blitch. I'll take the last two hours and prepare breakfast. We'll get an early start."

Sven wondered how he would know when two hours had passed. He looked at the Big Dipper and decided to use it as a clock. After it circled for what looked like two hours, he wakened McGregor. For five nights McGregor did not complain. Sven decided his estimate of two hours was close to right.

On October 11 they floated onto the broad Yukon River.

"Row. Row hard," Lt. Castner ordered McGregor and Blitch as the current carried them downstream. "There's a town across the river."

In mid-afternoon they landed at the town of Weare on the north side of the Yukon River.

"Thank God," Lt. Castner said.

Sven looked at him in surprise. It was the first time he heard the lieutenant say anything about God. Sven thanked God with a silent prayer. They were safe, safe in a real town with people who spoke English.

Lt. Castner promised the host of a boarding house that the army would pay for their food and lodging.

That evening they enjoyed a well-cooked, hearty meal. For the first time since he left Haines, Sven slept comfortably and warm in a bed.

"You will need these," the proprietor of the trading post said the next day as Lt. Castner, using the army's credit, bought warm clothing for Sven, McGregor, Blitch, and himself. "You arrived just in time. The temperature dropped to ten below zero last night. The Yukon is frozen this morning. You wouldn't be able to row across. The ice is to hard to row through and to thin to walk on."

"You mean we won't be able to catch a boat to St. Michael?" Lt. Castner asked.

"No," the proprietor said and laughed. "The last boat down river left September tenth. It looks as if you will spend the winter here."

"Here?" Sven asked.

"I don't know where you'd go. It's 800 miles to St. Michael and 1,300 miles to Skagway. You will have to stay in Alaska, so it might as well be here."

"I want to get to Circle City," Sven said. "Is there anyway to get there?"

The proprietor laughed and said, "That's a long way, boy. The only way to get there in winter is to walk or go by dogsled. I don't think you'd ever make it. You are young to be a soldier, aren't you? You don't even have a beard to keep your face warm."

"I'm not a soldier," Sven said. "I am going to join my father."

"Wait until spring," the proprietor said.

Sven shook his head.

"You heard him, Sven," Lt. Castner said. "I don't like it any better than you do, but it looks as if we must stay here now. Come along."

As Sven followed Lt. Castner back to the boarding house, he thought about hiking to Circle City.

"May I look at your map," he asked when they returned to their room.

"Sure," the lieutenant answered, "but I hope you aren't thinking about doing anything foolish."

"Not me," Sven lied. He had become accustomed to lying. He didn't feel his cheeks flush as they once had.

He studied the map. If he could make it from town to town along the Yukon River, he could get to Circle City. There had to be a way.

———

The next morning Sven slipped his four smallest nuggets from his leather pouch and returned to the trading post.

"I want to buy snowshoes," he said, "and fur-lined clothes like the Athabascan wear."

"Do you have money?" the proprietor asked.

"Gold."

"Where did you get gold?"

"I panned it. I'll give you a nugget for snowshoes and a nugget for clothes."

"Let's see the nuggets," the proprietor said.

Sven showed the man two small nuggets and he weighed them on a scale.

"Mighty small. I'll let you have the snowshoes or the clothes, but not both."

"Either of them for two nuggets?" Sven asked.

"That's what I said."

"I'll take both." Sven took the other two nuggets from his pocket and handed them to the proprietor. "You drive a hard bargain."

"So do you," the proprietor said and laughed. "Now don't go trying anything foolish. You can't get to Circle City this winter."

"I won't," Sven lied.

He found snowshoeing awkward and slow, but he practiced. Each day, to improve his skills and build his strength, he tried to go farther than the day before. He snowshoed and waited for the ice on the Yukon to freeze hard enough for travel. He would buy food and start for Circle City as soon as the ice would hold him.

———

One morning a young dog followed Sven as he snowshoed. Sven knelt down and scratched it behind the ears. "What's your name? Are you a runaway like me? Where's your home?" The dog wagged its tail. "It would be nice to have a companion to Circle City, but you must have an owner. Go home. Get."

The dog ran back a few steps and Sven snowshoed away.

"You, Boy!"

Sven turned around when he heard the shout. The young dog followed him, and a man on a sled pulled by six dogs approached.

"That's my dog," the man shouted. "Are you trying to steal my dog?"

"No, Sir. It followed me."

The man stopped, picked up the wayward dog and dumped it onto his sled. "What's your name?"

"Sven, Sven Olafsen, and I wouldn't steal. Your dog followed me. I tried ..."

Snarling and yelping interrupted Sven as two sled dogs began fighting.

"Bones, Harper, stop it," the man yelled.

Sven stepped between the dogs and pulled them apart. "Quiet. Calm down. What's the matter, huh?"

The dogs obeyed.

"They want to run, not stand around," the man said. "What did you say your name was?"

"Sven Olafsen."

"You're good with dogs, are you?"

"My father says I have a way with animals."

"How would you like to help with my dogs?"

"I would love to, Sir, but I am going to Circle City to find my father."

"Don't call me sir." The man pulled off his glove and held out his hand. "My name is William Cram. My friends call me Cram. If you will help with my dogs, I will take you to Rampart with me. I plan to go there when the river freezes hard enough for my dogs and sled."

Rampart, Sven thought; that's closer to Circle City. He pulled off his glove and shook Cram's hand. "It's a deal."

25

"SVEN, we'll leave for Rampart in the morning," Cram said as they returned from sledding one day. "The ice is thick enough."

"Tomorrow? What will I tell Lieutenant Castner?"

"That's up to you. I want to leave early, at first light. It's sixty miles. If you are not here when it's light enough to see, I'll leave without you."

"I'll be here."

Sven snowshoed back to the cabin. He knew what to expect. Lt. Castner would sit at the table, writing reports and drawing maps. McGregor and Blitch would be playing cards, the same as every day for two weeks. Blitch would ask to see his gold.

"So, Sven, helping with the dogs again?" McGregor asked as he entered the cabin.

"It is better than sitting here."

"Stupid, if you ask me," Blitch said, "staying out in the cold. Of course, if you freeze to death, there will be more room for us and we will have your gold." He laughed cruelly.

It was crowded. A barrel stove took up the end of the cabin opposite the door. Table and chairs stood in the center of the room. Two cots lined each side wall.

An idea popped into Sven's head. "I won't freeze,

Blitch, and you will never get my gold. You won't freeze either if you ever decide to do anything but sit. And don't be sad tomorrow when I'm not here. Mr. Cram asked me to move in with him."

"Good riddance," Blitch said.

"Don't listen to Blitch," Lt. Castner said. "You are welcome here; you are one of us. Stay here."

"Don't go," McGregor said. "You ought to know that Blitch is only happy when he complains. He will be sad if you ..."

"No I won't," Blitch interrupted.

"... leave us, and so will I."

"I told Mr. Cram I would move in with him." Sven took off his fur-lined parka as they talked. He took his pack from beneath his cot and began packing anything he did not need to wear in the morning.

"I hope you change your mind, Sven," Lt. Castner said when he blew out the lantern that night. "I can't order you to stay. If I could, I would. You are one of us."

"I'll think about it, Sir."

Sven lay on his cot. He hated the thought of leaving Mac and the lieutenant; Lt. Castner had become a friend. But he would gladly leave Blitch. Most of all, he wanted to find his father.

Fearful of falling asleep, Sven wondered how he would know when it was morning. When he heard the steady breathing of the men he tiptoed to the door and looked out. He noted the position of the big dipper. Six hours, he thought, I'll wait six hours. He lay down. To stay awake he thought of home, of what he might be doing on the farm if the family had not moved to Seattle. Tears seeped from his eyes as he thought of his mother, brother, and sisters.

Sven sat up with a start. Blitch stood in the center of the room staring at him. Sven stared back.

After a few seconds Blitch sighed, laid a knife on the table, and crawled back under the blankets on his cot.

My gold, Sven thought, he was after my gold. I have to leave now, before I fall asleep again.

Why had he fallen asleep? Through the oiled paper window it looked light outside. He hurried to the door. Pale yellow-green light, stretching across the sky in waving curtains, brightened the night.

Sven sighed in relief as he enjoyed the display of northern lights. Through the misty veil of light he located the big dipper. Four hours had slipped past.

Wide awake and chilled, he closed the door. He watched Blitch as he dressed, and as he tied his caribou skins and blanket onto his pack.

Holding his hand over McGregor's mouth, Sven gently shook him. "Mac, wake up," he whispered.

"Huh," McGregor mumbled and pushed at Sven's hand.

"Shh, don't wake the lieutenant. I couldn't leave without telling you. I am going to Rampart today with Mr. Cram, at first light."

"What?"

"I am leaving with Mr. Cram. I have to find my father. Say goodbye to Lieutenant Castner for me."

"Don't go. I'll ..."

"I'm going. Please don't tell until after we're gone, and thanks, Mac, thanks for being my friend." He grabbed his pack, and slipped out the cabin door.

Snow crunched under his feet as he walked to Mr. Cram's cabin. A light glowed through the window so he rapped softly on the door.

"Right on time," Cram said as he opened the door. "Come in and have some hotcakes. You can't travel on an empty stomach."

"Thank you." Sven took off his parka and sat down. In his excitement he had not thought about food. He ate quickly.

"You ride for awhile," Cram said as they harnessed the dogs and hitched them to the tow line. "The dogs are used to your weight and I don't want them to run so fast they tire themselves out."

Sven wrapped his caribou skins around him, sat, and leaned against the packs behind him.

"Mush," Cram called and gave the sled a push. The dogs, feeling the movement, strained forward and ran.

Twinkling stars and the white snow brightened the moonless night as the aurora faded. As the dogs turned upriver toward Rampart, Cram stepped onto the sled runners. Lulled by the steady patter of dogs' feet and the sound of sled on snow, Sven dozed.

———

"Whoa."

Sven awakened as Cram halted the dogs. The long northern dawn lightened the sky. Sven stood up and stretched.

"Time for a break," Cram said. He took dried fish from a pack on the sled.

Sven helped feed the dogs. The dogs snapped up their fish, gobbled them down, and curled up and napped.

"Here. You better eat too." Cram handed Sven a piece of smoked salmon. "It's your turn to drive."

"My turn?"

"You didn't think you were riding all the way, did you?" Cram asked. "It is my turn to nap. Wake me up when you get tired."

Sven walked down the line of dogs, petting each one, letting it know who was master for the next part of the trip. With Cram on the sled, he gave the sled a push and yelled, "Hike. Mush." The dogs surged forward.

Sven studied the shoreline as he drove. The broad white expanse of the Yukon valley surrounded him; even the trees glistened white with snow and hoarfrost. Though Cram rode the sled and the dogs pulled, Sven felt alone in the silent white desert. The shoreline guided him and only occasionally did he call "Gee" or "Haw," to turn the dogs on a bend of the river.

He watched the sun peek over the horizon and skim slowly across mountain tops far to the south.

"It's noon," Cram said, and Sven wondered how long he had been awake. "We'd better stop for lunch. Cut over to those trees."

"Gee," Sven called and the dogs turned right.

"Whoa." He stopped the dogs at the river bank.

"Good driving, Sven." Cram patted him on the back. "You feed the dogs and I'll light a fire."

Sven fed each dog another dried fish as Cram collected dry wood from the trees. "Fill this pot with snow," Cram ordered as he lit the fire.

Sven set the pot into the fire. As soon as the snow melted, they gave the dogs water. Three pots of snow provided water for all the dogs. Cram threw coffee into the fourth pot for them to drink with dry biscuits and smoked salmon. Sven ate greedily.

Sven rode until the sun set and drove in the twilight. Cram took over again in the early darkness of the short winter day.

"There it is. Rampart," Cram said as they rounded another of the twists and turns of the Yukon.

Sven sat up straight and stared ahead. Dim lights from candles or oil lamps shone from cabin windows. "How far?"

"Hard to say," Cram said, "a mile or two. We will stop at the roadhouse and look for a cabin in the morning."

"What's a roadhouse?"

"It's like a boarding house," Cram said, "only you don't get a room. You can buy a meal and sleep overnight on a bench or table or the floor."

"Dogs first," Cram said as they stopped before the log building. "I'll stake them down. You feed them."

After caring for the dogs, Sven entered the cabin behind Cram.

"Food and overnight for two." Cram called as they walked through the door.

"Help yourself. Stew and coffee on the stove." A voice answered from a back room.

As they sat at the table with three other men, Sven said, "I want to get to Circle City. Do you know anyone going there?"

The men stared at him and laughed. "It's winter," one of them said. "Ain't nobody going nowhere."

26

"Any empty cabins near here?" Cram asked the road-house owner after breakfast. "I'm looking for a place to stay until the days get longer."

"Not much," the man answered. "You might find a vacant one out of town. No steamboats in the winter so there are empty woodcutters' cabins along the river. You'll have to look."

"Thank you. Let's see what we can find, Sven. Get your pack."

"I need to find someone going to Circle City."

"Stay with me until you find someone," Cram said. "Any cabin I find will be big enough for both of us, and it will be free."

Sven grinned. Free sounded good; he would need his gold for food and travel. "Thank you, Cram. Let's look along the river first. That way if anyone travels upstream, I can to go with them."

"Feed and harness the dogs," Cram said. "I'll ask if anyone knows of an empty cabin upstream. When you are finished, drive around. The dogs need to run every day."

"Ask if anyone is going to Circle City."

Sven carried water to the dogs as Cram walked into the village. After feeding the dogs, Sven drove them between the cabins and houses. Each time he met someone, he asked, "Do you know anyone going to Circle City?"

The answers he received were similar; "It's too dark and cold. Wait until February."

Cram waved Sven to a halt from the door of the trading post. "There's an empty cabin about two miles upstream. We'll move in there. I bought some supplies we'll need. Wait here."

Cram loaded flour, salt, beans, coffee, sugar, salt pork, and some traps onto the sled. "We will trap this winter. We can trade the furs and earn enough to feed the dogs. Follow me."

Cram strapped on his snowshoes and led the way. Sven drove the dogsled after him. They found the empty cabin nestled in a grove of spruce trees and unloaded the supplies.

"You start a fire," Cram ordered Sven. "I am going to set traps if I see any animal tracks." He headed up a small stream with the dogsled.

Sven collected wood and lit a fire in the small metal stove. As the cabin warmed he stacked supplies on a shelf and fixed a place to sleep. The only cot would be for Cram. For his own bed he laid spruce branches in one corner and covered them with a caribou hide. When it grew dark he lit a candle, set it on a shelf beneath the window and wondered when Cram would return.

He collected snow in the large pot and melted it on the stove. The dogs would need water. He cooked beans and salt pork in a small pan. He was hungry and Cram would be hungry when he returned, if he returned.

Sven was finishing his meal when he heard the dogs barking. He sighed in relief and hurried outside.

"Thanks for the light in the window," Cram said. "I got traps set. With some luck we'll have animals in a day or two. Help me with the dogs."

"Let me take care of the dogs," Sven said. "Pork and beans are hot on the stove."

He staked the dogs close to the cabin and brought them water and dried fish.

"That was good," Cram said as he finished his meal. "I believe I chose a dependable partner. Thank you, Sven."

Sven nodded, and smiled at the compliment. If he were staying, Cram would be a good partner.

———

Each day for the next week, Sven snowshoed into Rampart while Cram checked his traps. He found no one going to Circle City before spring. Each evening he welcomed Cram back to the cabin. While Cram skinned the animals and stretched their pelts out to dry, Sven tended the dogs and prepared the evening meal.

"Sven!" He heard his name called on his eighth day in Rampart. He whirled around to see who knew him.

McGregor and Blitch walked toward him from the trading post.

"What are you doing here?" McGregor asked. "I thought you were on your way to Circle City."

"Yeah," Blitch said and scowled, "I thought I'd never have to look at your baby face again."

Sven ignored Blitch. "I can't find anyone who is going to Circle City until spring. I'll leave as soon as I find someone to go with."

"Go by yourself, Babyface," Blitch said. "You think you can do anything. Why don't you prove it."

"Leave him alone," McGregor said. "He never did you any harm. Sven, don't give up hope. Lieutenant Castner is determined to get back to Washington to bring his reports to Captain Glenn. He decided to follow the Yukon upriver all the way to Whitehorse. That means we will go through Circle City."

"This winter?"

"Yes, this winter. I'll talk to him so you can travel with us again."

"Not if I can talk him out of it," Blitch said and sneered. "Mac, I don't know why you want Babyface slowing us down."

"I like him," McGregor said, "and he never slowed us down. Come to the army barracks tomorrow, Sven. I'll talk to the lieutenant tonight."

———

Dogs barking early the next morning awakened Sven and Cram.

"Something's bothering the dogs," Cram said. "Hurry."

The two pulled on their clothes and rushed from the cabin.

"Call off your dogs."

Sven recognized Lt. Castner's voice.

"Hello, Sir. Come in, the dogs won't hurt you. Cram, it's Lieutenant Castner. You met in Weare."

"Mr. Cram, I need someone to take me to Skagway," Lt. Castner said as he entered the cabin. "I've been told that you are the best dog musher in the area."

"I do fairly well," Cram said, "but my dogs aren't ready for that kind of trip."

"I'll get more dogs, stronger dogs, if you need them."

"We are entering the darkest and coldest days of winter. It would be best to wait until mid-February to travel."

"I need to get my reports back to my captain. They will be useful for any exploring and trail making to be done next summer," Lt. Castner argued. "The army will pay you well for your service."

"It will take a long time to break trail and we may not survive the trip."

"We'll be able to make it, Cram," Sven said. "There will be five of us to share the trail breaking."

"Not five, Sven, two," Lt. Castner said. "I am leaving Mac and Blitch here in Rampart with Lieutenant Bell. They'll catch a steamboat downstream in the spring and return to Washington. Mac talked to me, but I have no intention of taking you along. You should return to Washington with Mac and Blitch in the spring."

"Drat it all! You're not going to stop me!"

Sven's face reddened as Lt. Castner and Cram both

stared at him in amazement. Sven bit his lip as he realized what he had said. He had never sworn before.

"Sorry, I know I shouldn't swear, but I am too close to Circle City to give up. I'm either going with you or I will follow you."

"That's why he came with me, Lieutenant," Cram said. "I've never met anyone as determined as he is."

"Nor have I," Lt. Castner said, "but he won't be coming with us. We need to travel fast. Sven, listen to reason and wait until spring. Then you can decide to go to Circle City or return home. I'm trying to do what is best for you."

"I think what is best for me is to find my father."

"Sven won't slow us down, Lieutenant," Cram said. "He is good with the dogs and could help us."

"He's not coming."

"Then we are not going," Cram said and winked at Sven. "I won't go without my partner. Goodbye, Lieutenant." He opened the door so Lt. Castner could leave.

Sven saw the look of surprise crossing the lieutenant's face.

"Come and see me at the barracks, Cram," Lt. Castner said as he left the cabin. "Maybe we can work something out."

"I think you will get your wish, Sven," Cram said as they ate breakfast. "Your lieutenant is anxious to get to Skagway. It will be a long difficult trip to make at this time of the winter. Are you sure you want to go?"

"I am."

"I will see what kind of a bargain I can make with the lieutenant. You stay here."

―――――――

The day dragged by as Sven waited. He stepped outside when he heard the dogs returning.

"Are we going?" he asked as Cram stopped the sled.

Cram grinned. "The day after tomorrow. I'll run the trap line and pick up traps tomorrow. You will stay here and pack. We'll go into Rampart tomorrow evening and stay at the army barracks. In two days we'll be on our way."

27

"HIKE, Mush," Sven called to the three dogs hitched to Cram's sled. He pushed the sled, with Lt. Castner riding in it, to start it, and stepped onto the ends of the runners. In the black of early morning he could see Cram ahead, silhouetted against the snow.

Cram drove a team of seven dogs, three of his own and the four best dogs that could be bought in Rampart. Cram's large cargo sled held their tent and stove and supplies for their trip.

Lt. Castner rode until Cram's sled bogged down in deep snow on the frozen river.

"Our dogs won't make it if they need to push through this snow," Cram said. "Do you want to turn back before we get too far?"

"Let me go first, I'm not carrying a heavy load," Sven said.

"Those dogs are not strong enough to break trail," Cram said. "We'll have to go back unless ..."

"Unless what?" Lt. Castner asked when Cram did not finish his sentence.

"Unless you break trail on snowshoes, Lieutenant."

"I can do that. I must deliver my reports." Lt. Castner strapped on his snowshoes and walked in front of Cram's dogs.

That first day they traveled thirty miles and camped in a cabin.

———

"Let me take the sled," Lt. Castner said as they stopped for lunch the next day. "You can break trail."

Cram agreed. For an hour he snowshoed in front of the dog team.

Sven, following, watched in amusement as Lt. Castner mushed the dogs forward with little success. The dogs did not obey the lieutenant.

"Calm down, Sir," Sven said when they stopped to rest. "You are yelling so much the dogs don't know what to do."

"Sven's right," Cram said. "The dogs will follow the trail. You need to relax and let them have their way."

The advice did not help. After three failures in three days, Lt. Castner quit trying. "Cram, I'll break trail and leave the mushing to you," he said. "Your dogs and I will be less frustrated, and I won't slow us down."

———

On December 13 they reached Ft. Hamlin, eighty miles from Rampart. The next day they reached the mouth of the Dall River where seventeen steamboats bound for Dawson were wintered in. From merchants on the boats, Lt. Castner bought enough supplies to reach Ft. Yukon, 220 miles further up the river.

Those 220 miles challenged their endurance and skills. Where the terrain along the river flattened, the river divided into channels and was more than a mile wide. Daylight lasted only two hours. The snow, three feet deep, reflecting starlight and aurora, brightened the night as they mushed onward in the semi-darkness.

In subzero cold, snow crunched beneath feet and sled runners, and breath froze in the men's beards and around the dog's nostrils. Sven and Cram's fingers froze as they broke ice from the dogs' paws or lit the stove to melt snow. Water froze almost as quickly as they removed it from the fire. In his efforts to stay warm, Sven ran behind the sled on his snowshoes.

If they found no wood cutter's cabin, they camped in spruce thickets for protection from the wind. They set their small tent in a space where they had trampled down the snow. Using two logs inside the tent as a base for their cooking stove, they melted snow and cooked food for the dogs, dried fish or bacon with oatmeal, rice, or cornmeal. After feeding the dogs they cooked their own meals of bacon or canned meat, beans, and warm tea.

They used spruce branches covered by a blanket and bear fur for beds. Wearing caribou skin socks and parkas, with the fur turned in to warm their bodies, they lay under blankets and wolf skin robes and tried to sleep. When they needed additional heat, they took the dogs into the tent to lay on top of them. Usually the dogs slept inside the tent's storm door or out in the snow.

———

Lt. Castner ordered a rest on Christmas Day. They stayed in a wood cutter's cabin and nursed their sore feet and slightly frozen cheeks and fingers.

Sven enjoyed the relative warmth of the cabin. Though he could see his breath condense, the warm water in which he soaked his feet did not freeze. Relaxed, he spent most of the day lying down, napping. He braved the subzero temperatures only to help Cram feed the dogs and rub salve on the dogs' sore feet.

Three days later they reached Ft. Yukon, on the northernmost bend on the Yukon River. They stayed at the village roadhouse three days, resting the dogs, and healing their own sore feet and frostbite.

"Do you know Olaf Olafsen? Have you ever heard

anything about him?" Sven asked each person at the roadhouse and those he met at the trading post.

The answers were all similar; "Who? Never heard of him."

"I'm ready," Sven said when Lt. Castner ordered their departure. "The next village is Circle City."

———

On January 5, 1899, the three mushed into Circle City. Sven did not know if he should laugh or cry; he had expected to be there in June.

It had been nine months since he ran away from his mother in Seattle; seven months since he had left Knik with Lt. Castner to find or cut a trail to Circle City; four months since they had crossed the Tanana River for the "short" trip up the Volkmar River and over the hills to Circle City. He sighed. Finally. Finally he had arrived in Circle City. His quest was almost complete. He would find his father soon.

Lt. Castner, after asking directions, led Sven and Cram to the army post at the edge of the village.

"Lieutenant Castner reporting, Sir," he said as he stood before Capt. Wilds P. Richardson of the 8th Infantry, and commander of all the United States military in Alaska. "My companions are William Cram and Sven Olafsen. Cram has led us from Rampart. Sven has been with me from Seattle."

"Where did you come from?" the captain asked.

Lt. Castner recounted the story of his adventures for the captain, and added, "I believe I should deliver my reports to Captain Glenn as quickly as possible. They will benefit those who come this year."

"I agree," Capt. Richardson said. "Rest up. I'll order supplies for you. Your trip will be easier from here. You should find a cabin or steamboat to stay in every night between here and Skagway."

"That is welcome news, Sir," Lt. Castner said. "We can lighten our loads and travel faster."

"You will find room in the officers' quarters for you and your men, or should I say man and boy?" the captain said. "Why is this young fellow with you anyway? Is he a soldier?"

"No, I'm looking for my father," Sven answered. "He is here in Circle City."

"Olafsen? Is that your name?"

"Yes, Sir. Do you know my father?"

"I thought that name sounded familiar." Capt. Richardson said. "Is your father named Olaf?"

"Yes, Sir. Where is he?"

"I haven't seen him in a few months. He has a mining claim on a stream about five miles from here. He came into the trading post about every two months. Someone ought to know if he is still here. Ask at the trading post."

"I knew I would find him!" Sven shouted in his excitement and hugged Lt. Castner around the waist. "Thank you, Lieutenant. Thank you, Cram. Thanks for taking me with you."

Lt. Castner smiled. "As if you gave me any choice, Sven. Now we shall soon be parting. After all we have been through together I will miss you, but I am happy we found your father."

"So am I," Cram said and patted Sven on the back. "You have been a great help to me."

"So let's find a place in the barracks," Lt. Castner said, "and then find your father. Thank you, Captain." He saluted.

"Dismissed," Capt. Richardson saluted and smiled. "It is a pleasure to see happy faces in the middle of winter."

"If your father is not here I'll sled you to his cabin," Cram said as they walked to the barracks.

"And I'll go along," Lt. Castner said. "After our adventures together, I want to meet your father. He must be something special to have a son like you."

"Thank you both," Sven answered. "I am sure he would like to meet you too."

———

"Sir, do you know Olaf Olafsen?" Sven asked the proprietor of the trading post.

"Yeah, I do," the man said. "Why do you want to know?"

"I'm his son. Where can I find him?"

"I'm afraid you're too late for that. He paid his bills in early July. Said he was going back to his wife and children in Seattle."

Sven's face saddened and tears welled up in his eyes.

"I'm sorry," the man said as Sven turned away.

Sven felt Lt. Castner's arm around his shoulder as he sobbed. The lieutenant guided him out into the freezing air where tears froze on his cheeks.

28

"WHAT do you think, Cram?" Lt. Castner said as he walked with an arm around Sven. "Can we convince this young man to go with us to Skagway?" He winked at Cram.

"I don't know. He only wanted to go this far." Cram grinned as he patted Sven on his shoulder. "I could use help with the dogs the rest of the way. I say we take him with us."

"So do I," Lt. Castner said. "Nobody would miss him here." He squeezed Sven's shoulder.

Sven grinned through his sobs. He was going home.

———

After five days, rested and resupplied, they resumed their journey on January 10. In spite of below zero temperatures, they sledded steadily each day. On January 17 they stopped in Eagle, their last stop in Alaska before entering Canada. Three days later they reached the Royal Canadian Mounted Police Post at Ft. Cudahy.

On a hardpacked trail, the dogs, pulling their light sled loads, ran steadily. Each night they stayed in a deserted cabin or at a roadhouse. Twice they stayed at Mounted Police Posts which were located every fifty miles along the trail. On January 22 they arrived in Dawson City, 330 miles from Circle City,

In that busy center of the gold rush, Sven stared at the sights of a modern city of electric lights and theaters. He had seen nothing like it since leaving Seattle. The crowds of people jostling in the streets and general store surprised him.

"We'll stay here a few days and rest," Lt. Castner said. "The dogs need it and I need it. My feet are sore." While Cram and Sven rode the sled runners, he had walked most of the way from Rampart.

"You should ride the sled more, Sir," Sven said, "now that we have a trail and the sleds are lighter."

"Maybe we should tie him in a sled, huh, Sven?" Cram asked and grinned. "We could travel faster."

"I thought I was in command," Lt. Castner said and smiled. "I say we stay here and rest."

He rented a room for them in a boarding house.

For the next five days, while Lt. Castner and Cram spent the day elsewhere in the city, Sven cared for the dogs. He fed and watered them, brushed their tangled hair, and rubbed bear grease into their sore paws. The first three days he hitched all ten dogs to the small sled and ran them out of the city. In every direction he found cabins or tents along stream banks where men had sluice boxes to use in their search for gold.

Sven asked everyone he met, in Dawson, at the boarding house, on the trail, "Do you know Olaf Olafsen?"

"He was here," the barber said as he cut nine month's tangled growth of blond hair from Sven's head. "I remember him because he had some good sized gold nuggets. Two days after I cut his hair a Mounty found him wandering alone on the trail about thirty miles out of town. Someone knocked him on the head while he slept and stole his gold. Poor fellow. The story was in the newspaper. I never heard if the Mounties caught the man who robbed him."

Sven stiffened and tears welled up in his eyes as he listened.

"What's the matter?" the barber asked. "That kind of thing happens often around here."

"He's my father. Do you know if he is still here?"

"I don't think so. The story said he planned to walk to Skagway and work his way back to Seattle."

Sven sat silently. The cord around his neck and the pouch of gold nuggets resting on his chest felt heavy. He paid for his haircut with a coin Lt. Castner had given him.

That evening, after telling Lt. Castner and Cram what the barber had told him, Sven asked, "When are we leaving?"

"You don't like it here?" Lt. Castner asked.

Sven nodded. "I thought you were in a hurry too, Sir."

"So I am." The lieutenant patted Sven's shoulder. "We'll leave the day after tomorrow. Cram tells me you have the dogs' feet in good shape."

"The dogs are ready, and so am I," Cram said.

———

Following the regularly used route, and with the dogs rested, the three traveled rapidly. A winter storm on Lake Laberge did not hinder them; it hastened them along. A strong north wind, blowing blizzard snow, pushed at their backs, driving them south. Nothing could have faced the storm, but it sped them forward.

On February 23 they arrived in Bennett City at the south end of Bennett Lake. The next morning they boarded the train at the summit of White Pass. Sven, Lt. Castner, Cram, and their dogs rode the last twenty miles, zigzagging down the steep slope, back into Alaskan territory and into Skagway.

———

"Sven," Lt. Castner said after arranging their stay in a boarding house, "I can't say that what you did was right, running away, stowing away, lying; but we have had quite an adventure together, you and I."

"Yes, Sir, we have. Thank you."

"I have some business to finish here, selling the dogs and seeing that Cram receives his pay. I have to go to the army post in Dyea for that. I would like to travel back to Seattle with you, if you will wait."

"Yes, Sir, I will." Sven grinned happily.

"Good. What are your plans, Cram?" the lieutenant asked. "Will you go to Seattle with us?"

"No, I think I will return to Dawson. It looks like there is still some gold to be found there. When I get paid I'll buy the supplies I need."

———

Sven waited at the boarding house until Lt. Castner and Cram returned from Dyea. Without the dogs to tend, he spent half the afternoon soaking in a tub of soapy hot water. The dirt of nine months and the chill of the trail slowly seeped from him. Clean and warm, he slide under the quilts on the bed.

29

"WAKE up."

Sven felt Lt. Castner's gentle shaking.

"Are you going to sleep another day? Cram's ready to leave."

"Huh?" Sven sat up and stretched.

"You missed dinner last night and breakfast. It's almost noon. Cram is leaving on the train."

Sven dressed quickly and accompanied Lt. Castner and Cram to the train station. Cram had five of his dogs back.

Sven blinked back tears as he knelt and petted each dog.

"Thanks, Cram. Thanks for helping me." He hugged Cram around his chest as Cram held him in a bear hug.

"Thank you, Sven. You have been a big help to me. Good luck to you."

Cram led his dogs onto the train and called, "Goodbye."

Sven and Lt. Castner watched the train chug from the station.

"Are you hungry?" Lt. Castner asked. "Let's go buy dinner and celebrate. A ship leaves for Seattle at high tide this evening and we will be on it."

"I am starved," Sven said and rubbed his empty stomach. His last meal had been yesterday's breakfast.

Lt. Castner draped his arm over Sven's shoulder. "Good. How does steak sound?"

He steered Sven into a dimly lit saloon, and ordered two all-you-can-eat dinners. They ate greedily.

As they ate Sven stared at a large black man who stood in the shadows near the door. The man seemed to be watching him.

———

"Two whiskeys," Lt. Castner called as they finished eating.

"Is one for me?" Sven asked. "I never drank whiskey before. I've done a lot of things I shouldn't have done, ran away from home, lied, swore, forgot to pray. I'm not going to drink whiskey."

He watched the black man walk to the bar and heard him say, "I's goin' ta serve da whiskey."

Lt. Castner said, "You're a man now, Sven, and after what we have been through, I want you to celebrate with me."

Sven shook his head and watched the black man coming toward them. He was big and strong and looked familiar.

"Drink with me, Sven." Lt. Castner said as the man set the glasses in front of them.

"Sven?" the black man repeated. "Skinny Sam? I's dinkin' I knows you."

Sven gasped. "Jefferson?"

"Skinny Sam? You's becum a man!"

"Jefferson? I thought you drowned. How did you get here?"

"I's swimmin'. I's lucky too. I's swimmin' to fisherman's boat. I's gittin' here in June."

"I thought you were going to Dawson to look for gold, Jefferson. That's what you wanted to do."

Jefferson grinned. "I's gittin' all da gold I's needin' right here. I's bouncer, takin' da drunks back ta der hotels. Wen I does, I's gittin' littl' o' der gold."

"You steal it?" Lt. Castner asked.

"No, Sur, Cap'n," Jefferson answered and laughed. "I's not stealin' no more. I's earnin' it. Dey pays me a littl' fo' helpin', so dey doesn't git robbed."

The talk of robbing reminded Sven of what had happened to his father. "Jefferson, did you meet my father? He came here during the summer on his way to Seattle."

"Maybe. Wat's yo' last name, Sam?"

"Olafsen. Did he stop here?"

"Olaf!" Jefferson shouted. "Sum'un's cum ta see you."

Sven looked toward the door where Jefferson was looking.

A thin, willowy man with long blond hair, a heavy red beard, and wearing a long greasy apron, stepped into the room. "Who's looking for me?"

"Dis man." Jefferson pointed at Sven.

The man stared and then rushed forward. "Sven? Is that you?"

"Father?" Sven jumped up and opened his arms.

As father and son embraced, Lt. Castner smiled and drank the whiskey he had meant for Sven.

Olaf held Sven at arm's length. "Son, why are you here?"

"I came to bring you home," Sven said between sobs. "Mother moved back to Minnesota. I knew you were alive, so I ran away to find you. We are going home. A ship leaves this evening."

"I cannot go, Sven; I have not earned my passage money."

Sven's sobs turned into smiles as he pulled his leather pouch from beneath his shirt. "I have gold. You are leaving with Lieutenant Castner and me, now." He pulled the apron from his father's waist and threw it toward Jefferson.

"Come on, Sir." He grabbed Lt. Castner's hand and pulled him from the chair. "You have your reports to deliver, and my father and I don't want to miss the ship. We're going home, home to mother."

AUTHOR'S NOTES

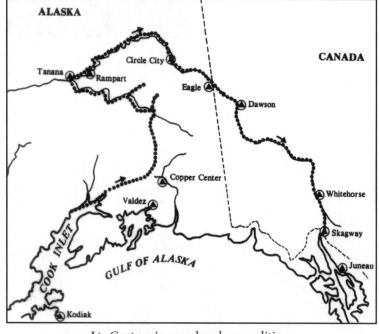

Lt. Castner's overland expedition
from Cook Inlet to Skagway,
June 8, 1898, through February 24, 1899.

HISTORICAL FICTION

SVEN Olafsen's adventures, though fictional, are based upon the true adventures of Lt. Joseph C. Castner, who arrived back in Seattle on March 1, 1899.

Lt. Castner served under Capt. Edwin Glenn in Alaska in 1898, as the United States began to develop trails from Alaska's southern coast to the Yukon River. With new trails, persons going into interior Alaska would not need to pass through Canada. Sections of the present day Glenn and Richardson Highways follow the route cut through the wilderness by Lt. Castner and his men.

Lt. Castner's autobiographical account of his exploration, taken from three sources,* is recorded in Lieutenant *Castner's Alaskan Exploration, 1898: A Journey of Hardship and Suffering*, edited by Lyman L. Woodman, Lt. Col., USAF-Ret. The book was published by the Cook Inlet Historical Society in 1984. Its Library of Congress Catalog Card Number is 84-70862.

The names of all military persons in this book were the names of real people, as were Dillon, Hicks, Billy, Kelly, Mendenhall, Chief Andre, Stephen, and Cram. Names of ships and mules are the names recorded by Lt. Castner, and the events recorded as happening to Lt. Castner are factual. Names of other characters, all character attributes, and all conversations are my work as author as I created Sven's story.

Douglas DeVries

Following are two excerpts from *Lieutenant Castner's Alaskan Exploration*, 1898: A Journey of Hardship and Suffering. The first tells of the hardship of cutting a trail through the Alaska wilderness; the second tells of the time Lt. Castner, McGregor, and Blitch came near to death by starving and freezing.

From page 15:

"No one who has not experienced it could possibly understand the annoyance mosquitoes are in this country. Our hands and faces were protected by gloves and netting, but, asleep or awake, eating or drinking, they find a way to sting and bother one. The food one has to eat gets full of them. We lived almost entirely in small tents. Getting inside, and killing all the mosquitoes, we sometimes got a little rest. Most of the men slept in a large conical tent, inside of which were more mosquitoes than outside. It was very hard to lead mules or cut trail all day, fighting mosquitoes all the time, then have to eat them at meals and fight them all night. The men were much dissatisfied and wanted to give up."

From page 50:

"On the 20th, 21st, 22nd, 23rd, 24th, and 25th of September we continued our painful march down the valley of the Volkmar, living on wild cranberries and what we called rose apples. ... For breakfast we gathered around a rosebush. For lunch we turned over the snow in a cranberry bog to gather frozen cranberries. We dined about 4 p.m. off another rosebush. Blitch had saved his tin cup, in which we boiled river water for a hot drink. Camp was made early to enable us to gather enough wood to keep from freezing at night. What was left of trousers and drawers was secured by ropes wrapped around our legs. In our effort to keep warm at night, we got so close to the fire that much of our scant clothing was burned while we dozed. From collar to trouser band the back was burned out of my shirt.

"Before this the cuts on our feet had become pus-running sores. Now we were almost barefooted, and dirt entering caused the sores to spread and fester. When snow covered the ground we had to halt frequently to remove it from between our toes to keep them from freezing. The rest at night caused the sores to close over, but we had to break them open in the morning to get relief in walking. Too weak, too cold, and too indifferent to care, we became coated with dirt, and great calluses formed on our feet, almost as hard as horn. ... Naturally we became very weak and emaciated in all our parts, as we were simply starving to death.

"Our mental condition was unsettled, and one of us added to the brain storms by having a faultfinding nature. We took turns at going slightly demented; fortunately all were not crazy at the same time. Every morning found us weaker, fewer rags about us, and our sores more painful. ... As my men often said, it would be impossible to make others understand what we suffered these days. No tongue or pen could do the case justice."

* "Exploration in Alaska," a December 9, 1909, speech given by then Capt. Castner to the Hawaiian Engineering Association in Honolulu.

U.S. Senate Report 1023, "Compilation of Narratives of Exploration in Alaska" (1900).

Publication XXV of the Military Information Division of the Adjutant General's Office in the War Department (1900).

LIEUTENANT JOSEPH C. CASTNER
US ARMY

LIEUTENANT Castner was born November 18, 1869, in New Brunswick, New Jersey. His career in the military began at Rutgers College where he trained in the Reserve Officer Training Corps. At graduation in the spring of 1891, he received his commission as a second lieutenant in the United States Army.

Lt. Castner was stationed in the Vancouver Barracks in the state of Washington when assigned to the Alaska expedition with Captain Glenn. His determination to succeed and reach the Yukon River, and to deliver his reports so that they could be used by expeditions in 1899, led him into the life threatening adventures recorded in his accounts of the expedition, and here in Gold Rush Runaway.

After leaving Alaska to deliver his reports, Lt. Castner rose steadily in rank as he served in the Philippines (1900-01), Hawaii (1908-1912), France in World War I, and China (1926-29), as well as in the states. His last promotion, to brigadier general, occurred in 1921, at which rank he retired in 1933. He died July 8, 1946.